THE
SHOOT

BOOKS BY ELLESTON TREVOR

Chorus of Echoes

Tiger Street

Redfern's Miracle

A Blaze of Roses

The Passion and the Pity

The Big Pick-Up

Squadron Airborne

The Killing-Ground

Gale Force

The Pillars of Midnight

The V.I.P.

The Billboard Madonna

The Pasang Run (In England: *The Burning Shore*)

The Flight of the Phoenix

The Shoot

THE SHOOT

a novel by

ELLESTON TREVOR

DOUBLEDAY & COMPANY, INC., *Garden City, New York*

1966

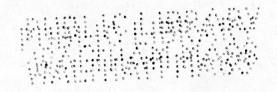

*All of the characters in this book are
fictitious, and any resemblance to actual
persons, living or dead, is purely coincidental.*

324972

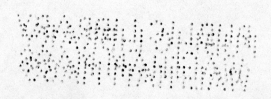

For Brenda and Morton

Chapter 1

The men waited, standing in groups, facing toward the east. The sky was starry and the ocean black. In every direction lay black water, glassy and soundless; the island seemed afloat on it, adrift.

Despite the batteries of instruments and the pools of light cast by the massed photoflood bulbs there was something primitive about the way the men stood, all their faces turned to the east, watching the sky as if they waited for the coming of a god. They had stopped talking minutes ago, and one of the guard dogs had begun whimpering, unnerved by their quiet, and the animal plaint made an eerie duet with the timing pips coming over the network.

When the voice started counting, the dog fell silent, comforted by the human voice even though it was metallic and came from nowhere. It counted off the seconds, and a strange mood came over the men: they began not caring, at this of all times; because there was nothing they could do about it now; it was suddenly too late and they were helpless.

Because of this mood—an onset of mental numbness—the voice counting off the final seconds became, it seemed, fainter, as the ticking of a clock seems fainter when there is no need to know the time. But they stood stiffly, as if the whole of the sky and ocean were speaking to them in this one voice.

The dog wandered, trying to find company, sniffing at a man's foot and moving its tail, looking up at a man's face, whimpering again. There was no response; it might have been wandering among the dead. Of these thirty-odd men, none was company for the dog. It wandered alone.

The voice had stopped counting. It had been the only evidence of anything alive. In this silence the smallest wave, meeting the shore, would have sounded even from a mile away; but the sea was still. The men stood rigid, held in the great calm. Then the white light came.

It was sharp in the dark, even at a distance of more than a hundred miles. Its blade lanced upward from the horizon and from it a track of reflected light came to lie across the sea. The men were suddenly on the move, released, and called across to one another from group to group. Many of them called the same strange word, in a tone of exultation: "*Tick-Tokariji!*"

Some of them laughed, for no reason; it was the tension breaking. Others told them to shut up, and the big kinetheodolites began swinging; but the voices went on calling across the calm air of the night:

"One up for Chapel!"

"Up she rises!"

"Tick-Tokariji!"

The guard dog was scampering from group to group, with every man its company, while in the east sky the blade of light seared faster among the stars, climbing in total silence. The voice began sounding again over the network:

"*Zero plus thirty.*"

Some of the men who were not busy at the instruments unslung their white composition helmets and put them on, moving toward the instruments to worry the operators with questions.

2

"Where's she making, Nobby?"

"Give us a number!"

"When do we duck?"

A big lens moved a degree at a time, its bloomed glass scanning the void where the white blade rose.

"Christ's sake shuddup, can't bloody well concentrate!"

The network sounded again:

"Point 331 degrees true. Will impact Zone Four."

The word was passed around and two of the recovery team climbed into the nearest utility hack and started the engine. Zone Four was six or seven miles down-range.

"Zero plus sixty. Fifteen thousand high. Prediction Zone Four."

The light climbed faster and was now more faint. In three minutes it had left the troposphere and the zero-plus-240 signal came through. Prediction had shifted to Zone Three.

"Make up your bloody mind," a man said and lit a cigarette. His hand was shaking because the noise hadn't started yet and he was always afraid of the noise, especially with a BJ-9. They were the worst.

The two recovery-crew men sat together in the high-built utility hack, their helmets gleaming under the floods. Zone Three was less than five miles away and they weren't going there yet. A shift in prediction to Zone Two would send them to the shelters.

They all still faced the east, watching the light of the missile. It would happen any time now: the noise. They would have to be looking at the light when the noise came, so that some of the shock would be absorbed by reasoning. They knew that the light was making the noise, so that if they looked at the light it would be in visual confirmation and they would feel they were in control. They always had to work it out this way and they often admitted it to one another and weren't ashamed.

"Plus four hundred. Prediction Zone Three."

3

The kinetheodolites swung on their gimbals. Talking had fallen away to an occasional word. The worst was over: there'd been no hitch on the pad; she was up and alive.

Then the network became filled with signals and they looked sharply away from the missile to stare at the dark blob of the P.A. speaker below the photofloods. The sweat began springing on them as they listened.

"Flutter setting up. Yawing—two degrees error."

"Bring in fives."

"Marked fluttering. Frank, you with me?"

"Skyscreens—what course?"

"Shut down at plus ninety—all yours."

"Frank! What do you read now?"

"Four degrees error—"

"Dr. Chapel?"

The men looked away from the P.A. and refocused on the faint spark in the sky: most of them were talking and none of them was listening; words fell about on the calm air; in the utility hack a cigarette dropped and lodged in the fold of a man's denim and began smoldering; he didn't notice until it burned his skin.

Then they heard the single unhurried voice.

"Cutting. Cutting."

Even those who had lived and worked here on 'Covery Island for five years had never heard this signal. It was the sentence of death.

"I'm cutting her down."

The light was very faint now, fainter than many of the low-magnitude stars, and its movement alone made it possible to pick it out. Then it brightened and became the biggest star in the sky. The explosion was silent. Its flare was acid and hurt the eyes of the men who watched, and on the face of one of them tears ran down, because of the beauty of the little death up there, and because of its loneliness.

4

The explosion was spreading, its bright stain swelling slowly and devouring the stars at its fringe so that their light appeared to feed its greater glare; then the fringe began breaking up and long streamers drew out beneath. The faces of the men had taken on a pallor, because of the far light; it was the radiance of sickness.

The P.A. spoke for the first time directly to them.

"Recovery team, take immediate shelter—immediate shelter. The missile is cut down. Danger of fragments. All personnel on 'Covery will take immediate—repeat immediate—shelter."

They moved across to the bunkers, not because they were afraid but because they were cautious men; otherwise they would not have been permitted to work here.

The noise came now. It was not the noise of the explosion but of the launching, and it had taken nine minutes to reach them from the main island, Tokariji. It had been traveling slowly across the curve of the ocean at little more than seven hundred miles an hour, while the missile had climbed at six thousand.

This sound was peculiar to the BJ-9. Most of the missiles on trial at Tokariji made a long-sustained roaring that shook the ground and pressed at the ears; it was nothing much to deal with. But because of its fuel and exhaust-duct construction BJ-9 had the note of a siren, or of a thousand sirens. Someone had said: "There's nothing you can do about it once it starts—you put your damned hands to your damned ears and it goes right through into your ears and into your damned head. You can't get away from it—there's nowhere you can find to go, because it'll go after you and get you. Once I tried screaming back at it, but I couldn't hear even my own scream—then I got scared, thought I'd gone nuts. That's what kind of a thing it is—it can drive you nuts."

Now they stood and took it, unable even to move. Far

in the east sky the explosion was dying away to a glow, and it was no good looking up there and reasoning it out, telling yourself that the glow up there was making this hellish scream. It wasn't true anyway. The missile wasn't there any more. BJ-9 was dead, and this scream was out of the past, the sound of something that had happened nine whole minutes ago and was over now. This was the scream of a ghost.

It came across the water to them and became the only thing in existence, bigger than the ocean and the sky, blotting them out as they stood with sick cold in their stomachs and their hands clenched as if they could fight such a monstrous thing with their bare fists. All the guard dogs, six of them, were yelping now, crouched back with their hackles up; but the men could not hear them against the scream. They stood in the gale of it and felt terror and could do nothing, nothing.

It lasted for a minute and a half, and then thinned out, but no one moved yet; they stood as if in thanksgiving. Then, when the first man spoke, some of them laughed at what he had said—they hadn't heard what he said; it was the laughter of madmen.

A dog leaped at someone and he held its front paws, slapping at the rough hide to give it comfort; the scene became human again and they moved off to the blast-proof shelters, their feet slow and uncertain as if the strength had been bled out of them by the scream. The sound was still there, a faint whistling among the stars.

They stayed outside the shelters, unwilling to go in until the last of BJ-9 was heard, so that they could give it decent burial in their minds. "Take immediate shelter" was just a phrase and they ignored it. Even if a big fragment were hurled directly downward by the explosion it would take minutes to reach the ground and its glow through the troposphere would warn of its coming.

6

A long time passed, in which they talked and lit new cigarettes from stubs, before the sound of the explosion reached sea level. It was not loud; the great distance had diminished it; but the air vibrated as if to the beating of muffled drums; and then the last silence came.

Minutes later the first big fragment struck the sea not far from the shore and they heard it and moved into the shelters, to stand huddled near the doorways listening to the patter of the debris outside. Some of the pieces, spinning in the air rush, whined plaintively before they hit the earth, and a man shivered, thinking, "Will that bloody missile never die?"

Half an hour, and it was safe to go outside. All that remained of the night were the quiet stars. They looked up at them. They were engineers, these men, practical men, but they worked and passed their lives in the vastness of sea and sky and were easily moved in their hearts, as city people can never be. Inanimate things were personal to them —a ship, an aircraft, these rocks, the sea itself. Above all inanimate things a missile was most personal to them; thus it was that the burial service was voiced without thinking, by one among them.

"That's it, then. BJ-9. Poor little sod."

Chapter 2

It took weeks to clear up the mess.

The physical debris was unimportant, though the men on 'Covery worked all hours, diligently combing the terrain of the seven main impact zones for the fragments of BJ-9. They were connected with the project, however remotely, and felt they must share the shame of its failure; their unremitting labor was purgative. Every day one of the helicopters took the gleanings of debris across the sea to the main island, Tokariji, sealed in polythene bags for delivery to the analysts. But nobody expected to find evidence of whatever had set up the fluttering that had sent the missile off course, forcing the flight safety officer to cut it down. The explosion would have obliterated every sign.

It was the mess in men's minds that took time to clear up; the attempts to apportion blame and dispel doubts, to take whatever action offered that might prevent another disaster.

BJ-9 had been on trial for nearly five years, and more than twenty of its type had been fired successfully from Tokariji, Woomera, and Cape Kennedy, with only minor modifications. Now it had failed and no one knew why. After the study of some five thousand feet of film and two thousand feet of tape there was no definite conclusion. No comfort was found in any one of the mass of technical reports that were radioed daily to London. A single line of the last page of the principal officer's personal report was the hardest to read: *I cannot, as yet, confidently rule out sabotage.*

The mention of sabotage was startling, first because Dr. Chapel was a scientist of an extreme order, devoted to facts, contemptuous of emotion; and the idea of sabotage was emotional in concept. Second, such an idea came readily to hand as a scapegoat when something went wrong, and Chapel was not a man to dodge an issue. That line in his report therefore carried more weight than it should, and people protested. The missile officer, Follett, told the P.O. in the senior mess, in the hearing of others:

"Even if anything had been deliberately rigged it would have shown itself on the telemetry, just like any other technical fault. We flew ten seconds after the fluttering set up, before we cut it down."

Chapel studied him before answering. He was never known to make an immediate reply. "People are saying that I suspect sabotage. They should read my statement more carefully. I said that I can't yet rule sabotage out. There is a difference."

Griggs, chief of Administration, said to Follett later the same evening: "How long have you known the P.O.?"

"Not long. A few months."

Griggs was a quiet man, older than most of them on Tokariji; a lot of his hair was gray and his slate-blue eyes looked unsurprisable; he stood balanced on both legs, short, thick-bodied, confident. He wasn't a scientist but it was said of him that his success as an administrator was due mostly to his understanding of the breed.

"Then take a tip," he told Follet. "Don't try to get at him, because you never will. He lives inside a triple-laminated shock-proof nickel shell and he's locked the door and

9

thrown away the key. When he wants you he'll let you know. And you'd better be there."

Follett tilted his head. He was young, even for a rocketman, and his scientific reputation was brilliant. Griggs knew that Follett was, in his own way, as difficult a man as the P.O. himself; but he was still young enough to be advised.

"I have always imagined," Follett said carefully, "that it's in order for a missile officer to discuss a project with his P.O."

Griggs had noticed how often the newcomers to Chapel's team tended to ape his careful speech, out of unconscious respect. Even when he had just given them a snubbing.

"This wasn't a project, old boy. This was a disaster. And when the P.O. has got it all worked out he'll be ready to talk. Then we'll really hear something. Now let's have a nightcap, cheer ourselves up."

He had been saying it all day, and all yesterday; he had been saying it for weeks, trying to cheer people up. It hadn't been successful. The killing of BJ-9 had hit them too hard. There hadn't been a missile run wild for six years and now it had happened. Half a million pounds' worth of intricate mechanism almost as delicate as a man's brain, hundreds of thousands of work hours and concentration at the modification and reassessment design boards and test benches, the physical creation of minds acknowledged to number among the most brilliant in the Western Hemisphere—and they were bringing home the bits in polythene bags, and no bit bigger than a lump of coke.

The depression had drifted down on Tokariji as if BJ-9 had produced a fallout when she had blown up. There was a kind of sickness on the island.

But there was one consoling thought to help Griggs in his attempts to rally their spirits. However long this depression would ordinarily last, it must clear by June 3. On that day, only a fortnight from now, White Lance was due to arrive. From that day it would go into preparation sequence and nobody would have time to think about anything else.

For all the importance of the BJ-9 disaster it had occurred to a minor missile during a routine minor shoot. The major trial scheduled for this year was White Lance, one of the biggest ever to be handled on Tokariji, and one of the newest. Often in the last depressing weeks Griggs had almost told them: You can worry yourself sick till June third if you have to, but after that date we'll be able to think to good purpose again.

But he hadn't put it into words. It would have scared them. White Lance was big and it was new, with a revolutionary second-stage solid-fuel cuckoo motor never yet flight-tested. They would be scared of it anyway; at a time like this its name couldn't even be mentioned.

Tokariji lies in deep ocean just south of the Tropic of Cancer, northwest Pacific, longitudinally in between and southward of Midway and Wake Islands. The nearest important landmass are the Hawaiians, a thousand miles distant.

The nearest shipping lanes run five or six hundred miles away, Yokohama–Honolulu northward and Suva–Honolulu to the south. The island is too remote to lend itself as a staging port for either ship or aircraft; the only traffic to and from Tokariji has actual business there. Its seventy-two square miles of rock and sand were uncharted until Lhengris took his deep-ocean expedition northeast from Australia in 1881; the only other record of the island was made when the U. S. Navy ship *Phil Wooster* drifted into the natural harbor in 1945, crippled by strong engagement with the Japanese fleet. The Americans, cheerfully turning misfortune to good account, took possession of the place, and ceded rights to the United Kingdom as a rocket research base at the time when Dr. Penney tested his bomb.

No one knows how Tokariji got its name, nor has anyone ever asked.

A hundred and thirty miles due west lies a smaller island that was never given a name at all until the first research team began operating ground-to-air missiles in 1951 under the auspices of the Aeronautical Research Establishment, Farnborough. A recovery crew, detailed to pick up the crashed remains of unarmed missiles from the smaller island, coined its name by usage, so that today it appears in the official records as 'Covery.

Two years later a concrete runway was laid down on Tokariji, running east-west and giving takeoff and landing facility of a mile and a half with a further mile of emergency break-off across flat sand and scree. Seen from the air Tokariji is roughly the shape of a revolver, with the runway laid along the barrel and the natural harbor (now dredged, walled, and equipped) forming the trigger guard. The new harbor is capable of handling vessels of up to ten thousand tons and has derricks specially adapted for the unloading of fragile shipments from the U.K. manufacturers of missile components, instrumentation assembly, and telemetry gear.

Again seen from the air, the revolver-shaped main island has just fired a "bullet" toward the west, and this is 'Covery, forty square miles of almost circular terrain, flat except for a few jagged outcrops along the south shore. The two islands are linked by radio-telephone and the services of two converted MTBs and three Wright Sabre-class helicopters, one of them adapted for night flying and both equipped for tropics operation.

Up to 1958, Tokariji had been used mainly for war-weapons trials—minor shoots with limited objectives. The administration was then switched to the growing space-research departments, and since that date no vehicles consid-

12

ered as hostile to man have been tested. Two years ago the first of the reentry projects was mounted, and specialist teams made their way to Tokariji from the universities and research establishments of England, Canada, Australia, and Western Germany, with free facilities granted for the visit of U.S. scientists and technicians, and with reciprocal arrangements giving similar access to Cape Kennedy and Vandenberg.

The three launchers on Tokariji were now geared to two main programs: high-speed reentry physics trials (for the study of reentry conditions encountered by capsules propelled back to earth through the subexospheric layers) and the trials of newly developed missiles, fuels, and ancillaries. Both programs were pacific, and it followed naturally that Dr. James Weyland Chapel was appointed to the post of Principal Officer, Tokariji.

Toward evening, when the horizon westward began turning from apricot to indigo and the sea darkened to jet, an aircraft lowered from the same direction and came into the circuit over Tokariji.

Dr. Chapel saw it from the windows of his office on the first floor of the Instrumentation Building and watched it land. It was half an hour before Mary came in, and she waited another ten minutes, leaning just inside the door, watching him, her level eyes half-closed and her feet together, her large hands held quietly, the one in the other.

The chalk scraped in the stillness; the mass of figures and equations so smothered the board that twice he had to rub out to make further room; the dust from the cloth drifted whitely through the light from the hooded lamp that was focused on the board. There was chalk on the elbows and cuffs of his jacket. Sometimes when he hung it up in the heat of the day Mary would take it into her own office and brush it as best she could; he never knew she did it, nor did she want him to know.

She leaned, watching him, until he turned and took up a slide rule from the desk; by the time his eyes were on her she was standing straight, her hands by her sides.

"Do you want me?" he asked. There was always the note of mild surprise when he said that, as if he couldn't imagine anyone wanting him.

"Sir William has landed, Dr. Chapel."

He adjusted the rule, half-swinging back to the board and consulting his figures. She thought: His trousers are too long. Why doesn't she tell him or do something about it?

"Who is he?" The chalk began squeaking again. She knew that to answer would be a waste of time; she had caught at the fringe of his awareness only for a moment, to lose him again. It was some little time before he asked again: "Who is he?"

"Sir William Collier, from the Foreign Office in London, Dr. Chapel. We are expecting him this evening."

Then he turned from the board and looked directly at her and she knew that with luck she would have his whole attention for a minute or even longer. The thought made her nervous, though she knew she never showed it. This mind, behind the dark-framed glasses and the thin-haired brow, had been brought to earth for a moment from flights of abstract meditation so subtle and sophisticated that their meaning would be quite beyond her, a million miles beyond her capacity to understand. And now this mind was devoting its whole attention to her, and almost she wanted to narrow her eyes as if against a blinding light.

"He landed half an hour ago," she said calmly, and knew already what he would say, word for word. The information she had so far managed to give him had been noted only subconsciously; consciously he had gone on working at the board. Now he must recap, and play her voice back so that he could listen properly. Was she ever anything to him but an efficient tape recorder?

"Sir William Collier of the Foreign Office in London," he said carefully, "has just landed?" He blew chalk from the grooves of the slide rule. "We are expecting him?"

"Yes, Dr. Chapel."

He considered, looking everywhere but at her level regard. Beyond the big span of windows there were lights coming on all over this part of the island as the brief tropical twilight gave way to the night. The three red beacons at the top of the radio masts hung like the illuminants from an expensive firework; below and across the harbor stood the silvery glow of the water-storage tank. Photofloods had sprung up brightly about Launcher 1, where the night shift were modifying the gantry in readiness for White Lance. The swept-back wings of the plane that had just landed caught an edge of light from the rangehead installations, taking on the semblance of an enormous boomerang.

Mary's nervousness had gone, because he was not at the moment looking at her. She said in her calm low voice: "He's waiting for you at the guesthouse."

"What has he come for?"

"To see you, Dr. Chapel. It's all I was told."

His eyes were on her again. "Why weren't you told more than that?"

"It's something special."

"They ought to tell you everything."

She felt warmth suddenly from nowhere. He said: "I'd better get along, then. Collier. I've never heard of him."

As he passed her she gently took the slide rule from his hand and put it back on the desk.

Chapter 3

The guesthouse stood within a few yards of the beach at the eastern end of the island, set apart by a long hedge of tamarisk that someone had troubled to plant; on the inland side of the hedge were the two long blocks of the men's quarters and the odd-looking Japanese-style house that had been sectioned off and redecorated in 1961 for use as the women's quarters.

The only buildings near the beach were the guesthouse and the senior staff mess, connected by a path of green concrete permanently sanded over.

Collier had been brought from the airstrip control tower to the guesthouse—a distance of two hundred yards—in the biggest staff car on the island, as befitted his status. Nobody from the Foreign Office had ever visited Tokariji before.

Eve Chapel had made his room ready and was waiting for him on the veranda, cool and bare-armed in the white dress she kept for occasions.

"My husband won't be long, Sir William. He's in the thick of something quite daunting but he knows you've arrived."

He thought her smile was rather shy, and that she looked young for the wife of a man of Chapel's experience; but then Chapel himself was young, and one tended to forget that. Collier had mugged up the dossier before coming out

16

here. The P.O., Tokariji, had worked on bomb-aiming devices during the war and had actually participated valuably in the "trigger" stages of the development of the first atomic bomb, at the tender age of twenty-four. Winning his doctorate in science in 1948, he had lectured for two years in nine countries on applied physics and had then turned suddenly and obsessively to rocket design. Four years ago he had opted to join the team whose task was to design White Lance, in the Black Knight-Blue Streak series; most of his high talent had been expressed in the creation of that vehicle. Two years ago he had put his name down for the post of Principal Officer, Tokariji, on the grounds that he would welcome experience of actual firing at the launch pad, since it would help him, as a designer, to study "live" conditions. The post had been given to him immediately.

Unmentioned in the dossier, but uncovered by Sir William's diligence during off-moments in his club, was the opinion that since, as a designer, Chapel could freely observe whatever live firing he chose—and as many as he chose—his grounds for seeking the post of P.O. masked a determination to take over control of Tokariji well in advance of the first White Lance trials so that he could organize things entirely his way. It was agreed by the more charitable that this move was less a reflection by Chapel on the technical administration of Tokariji than a reasonable wish to make sure that the White Lance setup was to his liking. The new missile, of an untried basic design and using an unpredictably powerful first-stage motor, was very much his baby, and he wanted to nurture it himself.

Two other opinions, again gleaned through the cigar smoke at Sir William's club, he tended to discount. One was that Dr. Chapel, never a sociable soul, had sought the remoteness of a Pacific island as a hermitage where he could work in peace. The other was that his wife had entered into a liaison with a man in the City whose complete ignorance of anything scientific she found refreshing, as the long-suffering wife of a human computer, and that Chapel had taken her to live with him ten thousand miles out of harm's way. Sir William, who had a loathing of any rumor approaching the slanderous, refuted this one strongly; it was thus the one he found least easy to forget.

She looked cool in her white dress—spiritually cool, reposed; and yet the smile she gave him occasionally seemed shy. Did she look the kind of wife who would make a liaison outside her marriage? He instantly rebuked himself for the question.

He had accepted a whisky and noted that she chose a tonic water in a polite gesture of joining him. She was glad he had enjoyed the flight and to hear that the London parks were already bright with daffodils. Her shyness seemed to lead her back and back into the safe harbors of small talk until he said pretty directly:

"You must hanker after London sometimes, Mrs. Chapel, living right out here?"

"I like wherever I am, wherever it is."

"Only a fortunate few can say that. Of course your husband's work is exciting. Do you share in it?"

"No, and I don't try. The mouse doesn't feed where the lion feeds. But I do what I can to look after the silly unimportant things. We've about seventy women on Tokariji, all young, single and married, and I'm their kind of Aunt Agatha when they want someone to come to. Then there's—"

"I feel sure you are just the right person, Mrs. Chapel, despite, if I may say so, your slight resemblance to anyone's aunt."

"It doesn't take much intelligence—"

"But a great depth of wisdom."

She took a sip of her tonic water, perhaps thinking of nothing to reply; but an expression of pleasure at his remark had passed across her eyes. Was she then unused to praise? He thought so.

"I'm sorry he's being so long, Sir William."

"The time is passing most pleasantly for me, but you must have other things to do."

"I told him I'd receive you. He wanted to be on the airstrip when you landed, but—"

She lied badly, he thought, and liked her for it. He said:

"He's up to his eyes, I can well understand. This has thrown a terrible strain on him, of course—"

"The BJ-9 thing?"

"Why, yes."

She nodded. "It's got all of us pretty low in the last week or two. I was so sad—I mean there's such a frightful amount of work that goes into those things, and so much is expected of them when they finally go up—you know BJ-9 was transmitting ninety thousand signals a minute, all valuable flight data, when they had to destroy it." The shy smile. "I'm full of random facts and figures, like a parrot."

"I'm certain your knowledge is far more extensive than you pretend, Mrs. Chapel—" and she sipped her drink again. "It must have been sad, as you say; and I wouldn't have liked to be the man who took the decision to destroy. Not your good husband, I suppose?"

"No, the flight safety officer. He was lucky to get off without a lynching."

Then Chapel came in quietly and quickly, brushing his thin hair back and trying to look pleased to see his visitor. "Sir William, I hope you'll forgive me—there was a problem we had to deal with and I had no idea of the passage of time."

Collier responded with an apology for taking him from his work, and before many more words had been exchanged he saw that Mrs. Chapel had quietly left them, and remembered that her husband had not glanced at her.

There was no time, until his plane took off the next afternoon, to concern himself with the Chapels' personal relationship—nor any justification, he told himself sharply more than once.

He spent only a few minutes with Chapel alone, first thing in the morning, and neither had time to waste in reaching the point.

"I believe you know why I was sent out here, Dr. Chapel?"

"Something to do with the BJ-9 failure, they said."

"To be more precise, Her Majesty's Government has received a protest from Communist China, claiming that fragments of your missile struck a naval vessel and killed a member of the crew."

Chapel considered this. Collier waited patiently. The sun, risen less than an hour ago, already cast a glaring heat through the windows of the P.O.'s office, and Sir William put on the dark glasses that Mrs. Chapel had thoughtfully placed on his bedside table.

"No vessel was struck," Chapel told him.

This time it was Collier who gave pause, and it was not his habit. "You are—" But he bit off the easy question. There was no need to ask if Chapel were sure. His brief abrupt reply voiced certainty itself, and Collier glimpsed the measure of the man; when the P.O., Tokariji, said that a thing was so, then it was so. "You are—prepared to make that your official opinion?" He changed the question, none too adroitly.

"It isn't an opinion. It is a fact."

"I see." They sat facing each other and for the second time Collier noted that the P.O. was gazing at something over his shoulder instead of at his face. The mild brown eyes were clouded in thought within the dark frames of his glasses. "Perhaps you could substantiate a little, Dr. Chapel. Even in London we like facts. As many as possible." He wished the fellow would look at him; it was like trying to talk to a monk in deep meditation.

A pause. "There is only one fact in this instance, Sir William. Since there was no vessel of any kind within five hundred miles of the perimeter of the fall area, no vessel could possibly have been struck." He had glanced briefly at Collier, and was now gazing past his shoulder again. It was all pretty annoying. Collier had been flown ten thousand miles here and would have to fly ten thousand miles back. If this was all he was going to get he might just as well have rung the fellow up.

"Of course you take all precautions during a shoot," he said, rather pleased with his little bit of rocket slang. He had picked up the word from Mrs. Chapel. "And of course my minister will accept your statement without hesitation. But in Communist China your reputation and integrity may be less widely known, and we shall have to present our official reply with a little—er—embroidery."

In a moment the mild gaze was transferred to Sir William's face. "Any embroidery will have to be done in London, and I must request a sight of the final statement before it's given out. Marginal notes by the uninitiated can only ever distort the facts."

The sun's heat aggravated Sir William's rising resentment. He'd come out here to get a statement from Chapel, much as a headmaster would ask some young ruffian whether or not he broke the window. The headmaster—or more precisely the entire Foreign Office—was now dismissed as "the uninitiated."

Yet it was clear that Chapel meant no offense. He merely had something better to think about, and it presumably lay somewhere behind Collier's shoulder.

"I shall be flying out this afternoon, Dr. Chapel, as you may possibly know." A gentle hint that he *should* know, even if it were damnably clear that he didn't. "If by midday

I might trouble you to let me have your statement in writing, personally signed, I shall take great pleasure in leaving you in peace." And the whole of the Diplomatic Corps turned in its grave, epaulets and all.

He got up. This move appeared to surprise the P.O. and his chair banged against the wall as he stood up, too, suddenly smiling. "I shall see to it, Sir William." He took him to the door, and Collier, in turning, noted that his rival for attention was nothing more than a schoolroom blackboard in the corner, smothered in figures that he dismissed as thoroughly messy. "What a long journey for you," Chapel was saying solicitously. "I do hope you won't find it tiring. But you'll have seen some sunshine, and a change is as good as a holiday."

Collier shook hands with him, sure that he would not be seen onto the plane this afternoon by anyone but the pilot. "It was sunny in London when I left, and the parks are full of daffodils. Thank you so much for all your help."

The instant he left the room he regretted having said it. He disliked handing out even minor slights. It was all highly odd: he should have left here furious with the fellow, yet his only feeling was of sorrow that he might have hurt him.

With the door safely shut he looked at the young woman who sat at the desk in the anteroom. It seemed much darker in here.

"I expect you're Dr. Chapel's secretary," he said.

"Yes, Sir William."

She looked intelligent. He remembered his sunglasses and took them off. The room and his whole world seemed brighter now. He said: "Dr. Chapel has been good enough to give me his time and I don't want to intrude further. But I *do* want all the information possible on the safety precautions taken here when the shoot went up. Perhaps you could help me."

"When the shoot was made?" She moved one of her

rather large hands, flicking a switch and speaking into the desk microphone. "S.O., please." She gave him a level glance. "I won't keep you a moment, Sir William."

"Thank you." He relaxed completely, sensing that he had made contact at last with the orderly world.

"Safety officer? I have Sir William Collier from the Foreign Office here with me, and he'd like a complete breakdown on the BJ-9 shoot from your side. I'm sorry it's short notice but he has to fly out at 15.00 hours today, and—" She listened a moment and switched off, smiling to Collier. "The flight safety officer is on his way, Sir William. You'll want to look at the relevant sections so I'll make out your pass and they'll endorse it at Security before you begin."

"That's more like it."

"More like what, Sir William?"

"I mean—thank you, you're most kind."

Waiting for the safety officer he was still aware of the room he had just left, and of the man in there behind the shut door. The door wasn't necessary; Dr. Chapel had his own screen around him. From their short and unsatisfactory meeting Collier had learned only that of all the information he had about the P.O., Tokariji, the rumors that had reached him through the cigar smoke were nearest the mark.

Chapter 4

They were twenty minutes in the security office and Collier left there with his illusions gone. This was no orderly world, despite the efficiency of the young woman with the level eyes. Tokariji was just a maze of high stone walls.

"I'm sorry about the delay," the flight safety officer told him as they began their inspection.

"The man has his job to do, I realize."

"That's what he's always telling everyone."

It had been damnably hot in the security office and Collier had sat and sweated, dressed more suitably for the cool April shade of Pall Mall than this hellhole.

The security man, who introduced himself as "Mr." Hurst, had been in no hurry. He sat looking at Sir William's passport and papers and was silent for five or six minutes. Then he raised and lowered his eyes three times, very deliberately, comparing the face with the passport photograph.

"Have you ever published anything?" he asked suddenly. His tone was quiet and the question was lightly put as if he were interested only in putting Collier at his ease; his guile was painfully obvious.

"A short appraisal of Sir James Brooke."

Hurst nodded encouragingly, his pale eyes fixed on Collier. The eyes were oddly flat-looking and red-rimmed, as if the man ought to be wearing glasses. He sat very still, a plump robin watching a worm. Collier declined to continue without direct questions.

"And what made you want to write about him?"

"He was an interesting man. The first of the White Rajas of Sarawak."

"I knew who he was, yes. And who published your appraisal of him?"

"The Mayfair Press."

"And what date was that?"

Sir William deliberately looked at his watch. "I have been sent here on Her Majesty's business, Mr. Hurst, and my time is limited. Since all my documents are in order I should appreciate very much your cooperation. The fact of my having published a minor book some twelve years ago can have no bearing on my bona fides."

"I've no information on it, you see." The pale eyes looked particularly bland.

"That isn't surprising. It was, I repeat, a minor book."

"You see, if I was to work only on the information I'm given, instead of finding things out as well, for myself, I wouldn't be doing much of a job, would I?" He gave a smile that positively sickened Sir William: it was a "knowing" smile, with the eyes suddenly aglint with self-praise for smartness and the fat lips compressed in pretense of amusement. "You understand that as a civil servant yourself." He slipped on his encouraging look, and Collier refused to comment. "Now, most people like you have done a little bit of writing in their time, even if it's only something minor; and it's easy for people like me to check on anything that's been published, so I'd say the bearing of this book of yours on your bona fides is rather strong. You say it was published ten years ago?"

Seldom had Sir William encountered such a bloody-minded fool, and it took him fully a minute to get himself under control. The heat in here was appalling.

"No," he answered vibrantly. "I said it was twelve years ago, published by the Mayfair Press of Queen Street at the price of twenty-one shillings, introduction by Wainwright Simms and foreword by Lord Meer."

It was twenty minutes before he was permitted to walk freely beside the flight safety officer across the range head, and the F.S.O.'s cheerful dismissal of Hurst as a "proper stonewaller" was not appreciated. Sir William would have more simply have called the fellow a bloody Commie.

"Miss White said you wanted to know about the BJ-9 shoot from my angle," said the F.S.O. "By the way, my name's Randall, George Randall. I can't take you into Control Center because you'd have to get past Dr. Chapel as well as Hurst, and that's never easy."

"I can believe it is very difficult, Mr. Randall."

"As you've picked on me and not the ground safety officer, I suppose you're interested in the precautions we take against anything gumming-up during the actual shoot. The G.S.O. is more concerned with unsafe procedures while the rocket's in its preparation sequence—when the bits are put together and when the fuel's pumped in, that kind of thing. Some of the stuff has to be handled with kid gloves, especially the fuels, and there's enough static electricity on this island to run a train, practically—you notice it when you touch someone or get out of a car sometimes, spark like a whiplash, have you noticed that since you came? That bunch of buildings over there are the technical units—telemetry, recording installations, digital auto computers, and analogue computers—it's where the rocket speaks to, feeding in a whole pack of data every second. My place is in Control Center when we're shooting but most of my information comes from the telemetry units direct. It has to be direct because a rocket can go off course within a couple of seconds and start a trajectory that'll bring it down across a shipping lane or one of the inhabited islands southwest of here—the Marshalls, or east—the Hawaiians—or even back on our own heads. That's why we need a flight safety officer. Have you any questions, sir?"

Collier wished he had brought walking boots. They must have covered a mile since leaving that damn fool Hurst and the ground was nearly all rock. Randall wasn't a tall man but seemed to be walking on stilts, the pace he could keep up.

"One or two," he said casually, hoping he didn't sound too much out of condition. "I don't understand why Dr. Chapel himself, or one of—of the team can't press the button that blows up the rocket. It *is* a button, I suppose?"

"Just a titchy button."

"They must know when something's gone wrong. Why do they need—"

"They need me because their job is to get that thing up and keep it going, sir. It's all they think about, so they're psychologically conditioned to doing just that. You know when you're in your car on vacation and your wife says there's a village here that would have a postcard shop, but you tell her okay there'll be another place soon and keep on going? You're conditioned to the steady hum of the motor and the long straight highway and you don't want to break up the rhythm. That's part of it. The other part is that for the team putting up a shoot the next village isn't so close—it's months or even years ahead, it's the time it takes to ship out the next rocket or even design and build the thing; and for some of them it won't ever happen at all because their university's only given them an X-amount of cash for their part of the experiment—a new gadget they've cooked up for assessing primary solar ray refraction or the centrifugal influence on spin-release mechanics, anything like that—and if that experiment fails, they've had it. Out of every hundred men on Tokariji there's five or six bastards—excuse me, sir—psychologically conditioned to killing every rocket in sight instead of getting them up, and I'm one of them and that's what they called me when I killed BJ-9. I see their point—they're very costly toys they pop off and they've done a lot of work on them —for them it'd be like smothering their own baby the minute it was born. My view is different; all I think about is human life and how lethal these rockets can be when they run wild; I just see them as a tin can full of dynamite and there's no hesitation when my finger goes on that button."

He gave a sudden smile that Collier missed because he was picking his way through rubble at the edge of an enormous pit that excavators were digging. "That sounds as though I've spent all my life doing it, but in fact BJ-9 was the first rocket I've ever had to cut down. It was awful."

Sir William glanced up at him, tripped on a rock, and decided to look where he was going. Cement dust lay in a haze over the ground here; they were walling in the pit with concrete, twenty or thirty men with a dozen machines. Randall pitched his voice against the noise.

"Every rocket carries the means of its own destruction, usually a small capsule of manganese dioxide that's detonated by ground command. The fuel decomposes immediately. Manganese dioxide isn't itself an explosive but it acts on the fuel as a catalyst and turns the fuel into steam, and in half a second you've got an amount of compressed steam inside the fuel tanks that would have blown Wright's railway engine clean through a mountain without disturbing the daisies. So that's my job, sir—if in doubt, kill it. It's no good just switching off the motor—she'd go on coasting vertically upward for a hundred miles if she was at full velocity through diminishing atmosphere and come down where she liked, plumb in the middle of Honolulu, maybe. Then there's the shipping lanes, too. Six hours before we make a shoot we're broadcasting priority signals to every ship in the Pacific, telling them what we're doing and asking them to keep reporting their positions so we can plot them and know where they are at any given minute. We've got radio transmitters beamed constantly to every major city in Japan, China, New Guinea, Australia, and New Zealand, with an automatic break-in system that'll put us right into any program that's on the air—but we've never had to do that, and it's only the biggest stuff like White Lance or the new—"

Collier picked his way gingerly through scattered gravel and glanced up, wondering why the F.S.O. had stopped talking. He almost prompted "The new what?" but realized in the same instant that the question would never be answered. Whatever the shortcomings of Hurst, security seemed tight on Tokariji, and Randall was not so careless that the full tide of his recital could carry him smack into an item of classified information. He was already swerving:

"Anyway it's mostly the shipping lanes we have to take care of and they're the only things that scare me. If a shoot ran wild and I didn't cut it down in time and it hit a ship and killed people, I'd feel I'd done personal murder. Ground's a bit rough around here—we'll get across to the range-head road and make back toward—"

"In the particular case of BJ-9, Mr. Randall, I assume that there was no ship within any area where you might have expected fragments to fall?"

"No, sir. No ship."

"And if there had been any ship in that area, you would have been absolutely certain of its presence?"

"Absolutely. That's my job. You see, once a rocket runs wild—"

"Yes, quite. Thank you." They reached the smooth concrete road. "What is the enormous pit they're digging, Mr. Randall, the one we've just climbed round?"

The young man suddenly smiled. "Say we call it a swim

29

pool, sir. Truthfully I don't know, and I guess if I did know I wouldn't be able to tell you."

Sir William felt a little happier; the advantage was his for once. He happened to know from contacts on the periphery of his department that the civilians working on that pit were contractors for the Army. How many on Tokariji knew of this project? Not many, because even the flight safety officer had apparently not been told.

"We have to go around here, sir." They skirted a red-painted fence, inside which a very large radar dish was whirling to a low crackling sound. "High voltage—customers are requested not to handle the merchandise." They passed in the shadow of a gantry as high as a city building and Randall spent half an hour explaining it. This was the gantry that would usher White Lance into the modified launcher—"maybe a couple of months from now. She's being shipped in here on June three and she'll take six or eight weeks to build and fuel and set up." He stood gazing at the immense skeleton structure that from here looked like the Eiffel Tower. "And if I ever have to cut *that* one down, Dr. Chapel is going to lynch me without a trial."

Then they were off again and he said: "We'll go and drink some coffee in my office—you care for coffee, sir?— and I'll show you actual pictures of the precautions I've been talking about, diagrams of the self-destruction unit, maps of various fall areas, all the works. There's no time to show you much more out in the open and you don't want exactly a grand tour of inspection—is that right? The big silver tank's for water storage, that one over there, and below is the main part of the nontechnical section—stores, post office, small movie house, hospital, that kind of thing—"

"How far is it to your office, Mr. Randall?"

"Oh, just another step."

Sir William gathered his reserves. Halfway down the longest road he ever remembered having seen there was a shout and the hum of rough-tread tires and Randall dragged him onto the sand as a truck swept past.

"Don't you have hooters on Tokariji?"

"We use them for emergency alerts. They produce the sharpest sound you can get, so we disallow vehicles from using theirs." He steadied Collier, who was pulling a shoe off and emptying sand out. "That square building's the airstrip control tower, but you probably knew that."

"Yes," said Collier, tying his shoelace. "Don't you have hitchhiking on Tokariji?"

"You wouldn't see anything properly from a truck, just a blur."

"Of course. Do you have only coffee in your office, or are there cold drinks?"

"We'll stop off at the canteen, if you're thirsty."

"Thank you."

In another half-mile they neared a group of instruments and a man came out of a low cabin whose roof carried a swinging radar dish. He called to Randall and went back inside.

"You mind if we make a halt for a minute, sir?"

"I should be delighted."

Randall crossed to the cabin with his easy lope and Sir William followed. "Saw you coming by, George," the technician was saying. "Thought you might like to take a look."

Randall introduced Sir William and the man held out his right hand without looking away from his radar screen. "Nice to meet you," he said vaguely. "All right, George, you name it."

A single white spot was traversing the screen very slowly. Randall stood with his arms folded and checked the bearing, direction, and altitude grid. "Some bug you've got there, Tony," he said.

The other man's concentration was so fixed that Collier asked the F.S.O., "Is it a missile?"

"No, sir. It's an aircraft flying at very high altitude. Eighty-two thousand feet, way up into the stratosphere."

"Is that unusual in this area?" He looked back at the technician. The man was gazing steadily at the white spot, and the white spot was reflected in his eyes. He said:

"I've been here six years and it's the first reconnaissance plane I've ever seen over Tokariji."

Chapter 5

The unit had been ordered to report to Woolwich two weeks ago for "special duties." Beyond this the men were told nothing, but since they were installed in drafting quarters, inoculated, vaccinated, and issued with tropical kit they had a rough idea that they wouldn't see much of the Hebrides.

By the time they moved off it was rumored that even the C.O. didn't know their destination and that he was to fly them out under sealed orders. It may have been true, or it may have been that this rumor was designed instinctively to counteract frustration; for it was well known that if Colonel Pyne knew where they were going he certainly wouldn't have let on; he was a man whose mouth shut like a trap on anything confidential.

There weren't many places left in the tropics where the British Army had any right to go, but obviously they were going southeast. When the transport aircraft took off and set course due west across the Atlantic a new crop of rumors began among its passengers. It was now clear that precautions were being taken: they were "doing a Columbus"—making west in order to reach the east, because nobody in America or Canada would worry about them, whereas if they made southeast through Cairo, Karachi, and Singapore they would have to change into civilian dress at transit stations and make compliances with overflying regulations.

Within thirty-six hours the aircraft was enjoying staging facilities at Midway Island, where the United States Air Force contingent seemed to know all about them and threw an immediate party.

Early on the morning of May 28 the unit left Midway and arrived over its destination before noon. Looking down on the place as the plane made a circuit, Colonel Pyne remarked to his adjutant that it was shaped rather like a revolver.

"Christ, I hope Ken knows where he's got us!"

"I told you, it was sealed orders."

"Wonder we stopped in time. Break into a trot on this bloody place an' you'd be in the drink before you could shut your mouth!"

"Seen any talent, Joe?"

"Couple of blondes workin' one o' them kine's over there. Have to get their minds off the job, can't let talent like that go waste."

"What makes you think we'll be allowed to frat?"

"Allowed? It's nature, isn't it? Can't stop it. Nature's a pure an' beautiful thing."

"Look out, here's Ken."

For most of his company Colonel Pyne had the satisfactory appearance of a typical commanding officer, and they reappraised him as he stood before them in the bright sun, lean, hard, easy in his stance and steady in his movements. Some had seen action with him in Egypt and Cyprus, and revered him. Some took his confidence for arrogance and hated his guts. Between these extremes his detachment of thirty men unconsciously measured their opinion of him by calling him, among themselves, by his Christian name.

34

The voice of Sergeant-major Rice rang across the stones. "*Companee . . . stand't—haice! Stand—haisy!*"

The sky was hard and blue. They stood with their eyes narrowed in the glare. Those of them who had neither been out of England with their commanding officer nor had seen him on the Rugger field were today faced with a new dimension of him: his knees were bare. And for those who went habitually in fear of him, here was solace: a man with bare knees must be, if only in this small measure, human.

"Right." His head was up an inch as if sniffing the wind. "We now know where we are. We shall shortly know why. It's not an action theater. We are not in any way here in defense of this island, Tokariji. The island is under authoritative civilian administration and we are here as guests, in the peaceful service of the Queen."

He began pacing, hands tucked at his back. One or two of the men were looking slightly upward against the glare. "Since we are a missile unit, it's understandable that we feel a little superior to other mortals. It's incorrect but understandable. The weapons we are expressly trained to handle are the latest of their kind and they differ from orthodox artillery as a gun differs from the bow and arrow. Less than a month after my receiving the privilege of commanding this unit there was a public bar broken up near Aldershot Camp because certain of you chose to refer to an orthodox gunner regiment as the Bloody Roundheads."

Nearly all of them were now gazing upward, and the dutiful laughter was thin. Colonel Pyne turned in his pacing and threw a casual glance at the sky, where a silver-enveloped radiosonde balloon was rising above the Meteorology Building. In the clear air it looked strangely two dimensional, like a disk cut out of the blue.

"You should be warned that of the three hundred civilians on this island, some two hundred are scientists and technicians for whom our most advanced guided weapon has all the mystery of a brickbat. We shall find it refreshing to wear the boot on the other foot."

The shadow of the balloon was passing across the ground where they were paraded, and they gazed up at the artificial eclipse of the sun. Sergeant-major Rice waited now for the inevitable interjection, and had a fair idea of how it would be phrased: "You are permitted fifteen seconds in which to gape like a bunch of bumpkins at that pie in the sky and you will then honor me with the doubtful privilege of your attention."

It didn't come. Old Ken seemed as interested in the balloon as they were.

"Point two. Of these three hundred civilians, some seventy are young women."

Every head snapped down.

"Of those seventy, some fifty are unmarried."

Attention was absolute.

"There will be opportunities for social contact with the civilian population of Tokariji, since the senior staff mess has extended its hospitality to the officers and senior N.C.O.s, and the junior staff mess to the junior N.C.O.s and other ranks. I have warmly thanked our hosts for this very friendly gesture." He came to a halt in his pacing precisely opposite the middle man in the front rank and raked them with cold eyes. "With the exception of those two places, all buildings and installations are out of bounds. Casual contact with civilians in off-duty hours is expressly disallowed. Any member of this unit, of whatever rank, found in the vicinity of the civilian women's quarters will become subject to the most severe disciplinary action forthwith."

Bare knees or no, there was nothing human now in the figure that stood facing them. Erect, rigid, motionless, it might have been made of iron. The peak of the cap shadowed half the face and from that crescent of darkness the eyes shone like the eyes of a hooded hawk. Every man had stiffened.

"When you see these orders go up on the board, read them carefully and remember them." Then suddenly it was a man who stood there, instead of a dangerous machine. Pyne had folded his arms and the rigidity was broken. "Not such good news, I know. The thing is this: we are an operational unit away from home, and we are offered a hospitality that it would be easy to abuse. Further, this is a very small island, so that personal relationships lack the privacy afforded by the more dispersed environs we are used to. Any breach of good conduct would become general knowledge among the civilian population overnight. We have been accepted here for what we are—a company of gentlemen—and as such we shall one day leave here, with our good name intact."

The arrival on Tokariji of thirty men and their equipment went almost unnoticed. Apart from personal gear, all the equipment had already come in by ship during the past two weeks and had been part of larger consignments destined for the civilian scientific authority.

The civilian population was also preoccupied with its own affairs. In a few days the main components of White Lance were due to arrive.

The mood of the island had changed oddly since yesterday evening. Appearances remained the same: the senior mess was quiet and people went home early; the postal delivery was a popular event, as if they were eager to regain contact with the easygoing world beyond Tokariji and escape from immediate affairs; tempers were quick to flare and conversation was cynical. Yet the mood had changed from the subdued to the apprehensive.

Yesterday evening it was reported that Dr. Chapel had called in his senior scientific and technical staffs for a final discussion on the BJ-9 disaster—and had presented them with a verdict. He had been driving himself to the limit for three weeks and in the past few days had driven others: Follett, his missile officer, Randall, his flight safety officer, and the chiefs of Operations, Trials Control, and Telemetry Analysis. And the verdict was that a fault in the secondary autopilot system had been the direct cause of the failure. The system had been installed integrally by the manufacturer's specialist team, so that all responsibility rested with them. Conversely, no vestige of responsibility rested with the permanent staffs of the Tokariji establishment.

This verdict, reached by the P.O. single-handed, built upon mass data supplied by his officers, was examined closely at the meeting and was unanimously endorsed. It was now for the manufacturers of the faulty system to review their design and modify it and for the trials staff of Tokariji to lighten its heart.

Coming at almost any other time the mood would have lifted. There would have been a celebration. However sympathetic the trials people might have felt toward a manufacturer of repute who had for once produced a bad egg, they would have been ready to celebrate the fact of their own acquittal. Each of a hundred and ninety technicians had played a precise part in the BJ-9 shoot, some of them working within limits of one millionth of an inch or one ten-thousandth of a second, and none had slipped up. For them, BJ-9 had been a success, up to the point where a manufacturing fault had changed it into a rogue missile that had to be killed before it could do damage.

Coming at this time the mood did not lift. People stopped worrying about BJ-9 but started worrying about White Lance. Apprehension set in automatically and so fast that few had time to appreciate what Dr. Chapel had done. He had set out to trace the cause of a disastrous trial and nail it down before the next trial went into first sequence. If White

Lance had gone into sequence while responsibility for the BJ-9 failure were still unknown, the new trial would have been dogged throughout every phase by doubts. Chapel had known this; they all had known it. Now the record was clean, at the eleventh hour.

But there was no celebration. White Lance was a first-off prototype, untried and unpredictable; the potentialities— and the potency—of its fuel alone was fuel for apprehension.

Griggs, the administration officer, put the matter crudely but well enough in the senior mess on the evening of the Chapel report. "There's just been a bull in the ring that ran wild and could have killed off the whole cuadrilla. Now there's a bigger bull, coming in fresh."

On May 16 Sir William Collier had flown out of Tokariji with the principal officer's signed statement, with which Her Majesty's Government would counter the claim by Communist China of damage by negligence resulting from an operation under the authority of U.K. space research. Few were aware that Collier had left, or even that he had been here.

On May 28 Colonel Pyne's missile unit landed on Tokariji and the company was established nearby the now-completed weapon pit in the northeast area of the island. Their arrival was, by policy, unobtrusive, and few remarked it.

On June 3 the *Maid of Mersey*, an eight thousand ton merchant ship out from Liverpool ended her voyage of fourteen days to make port at Tokariji. Her cargo comprised the main elements of White Lance. Her crew were surprised to see so many people gathered at the dockside, and wondered at the strange silence that was over them all.

Chapter 6

There was an inlet, halfway along the north coastline of the island, and a slope of sand where the water never came. The place could not be seen from above, and she had found it by chance, passing close to the shore one day in the motor launch. Since that time she had come down to the cove often, making rough steps by dislodging the rocks. She had not told anyone.

The sand here was silvery, with shells and sometimes the skeletons of small fish; she had collected the most attractive ones and made a bracelet of them, wearing it always. A strip of still water lay between the sea and the slope of sand, deep enough for swimming. The first few times she had put on a swimsuit but had not bothered since; there was no path along the top of the rocks and no reason for anyone to pass that way.

Sometimes she lay, after swimming, on a certain rock of an extraordinary smoothness, and let her hair dry in the sun. There was a little round protuberance in the middle of the rock, and sometimes she lay on her front and dreamed there, while her hair dried and the water came slackly up the inlet, to gurgle among the hollows.

This part of the coast was always deserted; the main installations and living quarters were on the other side of the island, grouped around the harbor, so that in the cove it was possible to believe that there was no other life anywhere; and sometimes when she had dreamed intently she afterward climbed the rough steps to see with surprise that nothing had changed: the radio mast and airstrip wind sock and water tower were still there; and sometimes she wished with all her heart that they were not.

In her first year on Tokariji she had come to the cove infrequently, worried that someone would see her there. Now she came every day or simply whenever she could, and sometimes urgently.

Every road vehicle on the island filled up with petrol or diesel fuel at a pumping station on the dock, and Colonel Pyne took his personal Land-Rover there on the afternoon of his arrival. There had been some doubt as to whether road vehicles would be needed on Tokariji, but he had applied for an allocation of three utilities and a motorcycle and they had been unshipped with the other equipment a week before. He wasn't sorry. The area where he and his unit had their business was less than a mile square, but the few roads on this part of the island were rough, and the heat blistered the feet.

A small labor force was working on the dockside, rigging a derrick; he had been told that a ship was due in less than a week, bringing a missile for the civilian authority. Except for these few men the dock was lifeless, and even the water seemed pressed flat by the sun's heat. He watched the man at the pump and noticed that he had grounded the nozzle of the hose direct to the metal body of the Land-Rover with a length of cable. There was a warning about static on this place, in company orders.

It seemed about all there was on Tokariji: heat, rocks, and static electricity. So far he hadn't seen a tree or anything green except the burned-up tamarisk near the senior mess. How long were they going to be cooped up in this Godforsaken hole?

"D'you ever get any rain here?" he asked the man.

"Rain? What's that?"

The petrol fumes were sickly on the air.

"Ever any wind?"

"Get a squall come up sometimes."

The man was like the others Pyne had seen since his arrival: morose and uncommunicative. Either the Army wasn't popular here or this was the natural character of the natives; there was also some talk of a shoot having been gummed up recently; maybe it was that.

A woman came up on a man's bicycle, halting near the Land-Rover with her legs astride the crossbar; she had plimsolls on and the sleeves of her white overalls were rolled up, and her face was shiny.

"I expect you're Colonel Pyne?"

He decided to let her have a brief salute. If there were any more like this on Tokariji he wouldn't miss the trees.

"I'm Mrs. Chapel." She gave a gauche smile.

"How d'you do, Mrs. Chapel."

"I tried to call on you soon after you landed, but an officer told me you were busy checking the shipment."

"That was uncivil of him." Her sense of style was fetching; did people really "call on" people in this outpost of barren rock?

"Oh no—he volunteered to find you, but you were down at the harbor, I think. Has all your gear come through intact?"

"Everything's in order, thanks."

The man removed the hose, bonded the nozzle to the pump, and hooked it in. He handed Pyne a book for signature.

"We should have met your plane," Mrs. Chapel said, "but I was down at the laundry where one of the machines has broken, and my husband obviously wasn't told who was arriving."

"An unimportant soldier. Your Mr. Griggs took me in hand most courteously."

"We still should have met your plane." Her insistence on formality was embarrassing. "Was it a comfortable flight?"

"Most enjoyable, thank you." He took a pace back. "If you'll forgive me I'll get the car clear of the pump."

He got in and started up and the man told him: "Always bond yourself when there's anything inflammable about, see? Give a quick slap as far from the tank as you can, so there's no spark." He slapped one of the head lamps. "We got static on Toka an' it's murder."

Pyne nodded and began driving off, but Mrs. Chapel was alongside, still astride her bicycle. "My husband and I hope you'll have dinner with us this evening, Colonel."

"That's most kind of you. What time shall I report?"

"If seven-thirty suits you, we can have a drink first. Please bring your adjutant, of course."

Three Nissen huts had been allocated to the company at the eastern end of the island; they had evidently housed civilian technicians at an earlier time; the walls were still covered in charts, instrumentation graphs, and blown-up pictures of missiles. There was also an embarrassment of furniture, and hardly a ranker was short of his own armchair. Colonel Pyne had decided to preserve the status quo: the men would have discomfort enough on this tropical rock and there was probably nowhere to put the furniture if they asked for it to be moved out.

Major Nash blew out a thin stream of smoke and used the ashtray. "Well, the boys are happy."

Pyne stood at a window, listening. Every window in the three huts was open and he could hear the men still talking. They had been taken down to the dock this afternoon to check their shipment, and were still excited. Their new weapons were six short-range ground-to-ground Javelin 33s and they had never seen them before.

"It was like giving sweets to children," he said to his adjutant.

"Wait till they see the Triton."

Pyne stayed another minute at the window. A little while ago the sun had touched the sea and set it ablaze; now it was night. Nothing was gentle about Tokariji, and part of his spirit was repelled by the brutality of the place, and part was attracted.

"Mess jackets?" asked Nash. He got up unwillingly; it was time to change. The nights here were going to be hot.

"Of course." Pyne came away from the window. "Mrs. Chapel would expect it."

"Like that, is she?"

"I can't say what she's like. An old-fashioned kind of child."

Nash paused in the doorway between their rooms. "Child?"

"Oh, I suppose she's thirty, but there's something shy about her."

"Shy? Oh, Jesus. What a place to be shy in."

"It may not be the word I want."

"You shouldn't have dressed up," she said.

"I'm sorry?"

"You look so grand."

She had put on her white dress, the one for occasions, but Jim would arrive straight from his office and she should have told them it was informal.

Colonel Pyne and his adjutant stood side by side, each with a drink in hand. Nash found himself thinking: "Now that she's got us here she doesn't know what to do with us."

He could feel the emanation of Pyne's boredom already and knew he'd start hitting the Scotch.

"You live in a charming house, Mrs. Chapel."

"Thank you, Colonel. My husband had it built to his own design when we came out here."

The room was functional: the dining alcove was served by a hatch from the kitchen, the table being a precise arm's length from the hatch; the lighting was efficiently focused from clusters of metal-shrouded lamps above the table and the four armchairs in the main part of the room; two of the chairs were each placed near a case of bookshelves, one of which had novels in it, brightly-jacketed, the other of which was wholly filled with technical reference books, so that these two chairs lacked only a label: Mr. Chapel, Mrs. Chapel. The floor was tiled in plain squares of stone blue; the ceiling was a slab of acoustic composition material; an air-conditioning grill was in the wall over the door.

Yet the room looked lived in, Nash thought. Maybe it was the pink stole that had slipped half to the floor from one of the chairs.

"Do you find your quarters comfortable?" asked Mrs. Chapel.

"More so than we're used to." Pyne was deliberately toying with his empty glass; for the moment she didn't notice.

"The boys are in clover," Nash smiled. "Armchair warriors we'll have to call them."

But she was watching Pyne, and now saw that his glass was empty. When she brought the decanter he didn't stop her until it was a quarter full.

A girl with plump arms was hovering beyond the open hatch and soon Mrs. Chapel said: "Would you mind if we started without my husband?"

They sat down in silence. She was for a moment lost for small talk; Pyne, after three good measures of whisky, intended to leave any social effort to his second-in-command; and Nash was never good at it by his nature. He made attempts and Mrs. Chapel responded. Pyne said nothing, letting them get on with it. If the principal officer couldn't have sent someone to meet the plane he could at least have turned up on time for dinner, and if this young woman had any influence over the man at all she should have used it.

Sometimes he found himself watching her, his eyes attracted to the bare brown arms or the angle of her head as she listened to Robert, or the shyness—the implied vulnerability—of her smile. Her fair hair was cropped short and she was slender, yet there was nothing boyish about her, even in overalls riding a bicycle; there was, if anything, a girlishness to her, and he thought: "You're not my type." But he went on watching her.

Robert was doing his best, give him credit. His greatest weakness was a sense of pity. Whatever type this girl was, she seemed to be asking for help, so Robert was her man.

Chapel did not come in alone. Three men were with him and they went on talking for a while at the other end of the room, spreading some kind of blueprint across one of the chairs and studying it, one of them talking very fast while Chapel, particularly, listened.

Pyne watched Mrs. Chapel, interested to see what she would do. For her sake Nash began speaking more loudly, not looking away from the table, and for a while she listened, seemingly unconcerned about the bear garden (as Pyne thought of it) that was now established in the room. Then with a smile to Nash she left the table and went across to the group of scientists, saying something to her husband.

In her absence her two dinner guests looked at each other. "Poor little bitch," murmured Nash.

"She's not worried. But what the hell made her ask us here?"

The group was giving her immediate attention and one man was already going out; the other two followed and Chapel came quickly to the alcove, all pockets and turnups, smoothing his thin hair back, shaking hands first with Nash, who tried to stand back and make room for his commanding officer, too late.

"Colonel Nash, you must forgive me—" His left hand straightened his tie.

"No, Jim—*this* is Colonel *Pyne*—"

"Oh, I see—"

"How d'you do, sir?"

"And Major Nash—"

"Oh yes—"

"I knew you wouldn't mind our starting—"

"But of course—" He sat down in his wife's place and she simply took her half-finished plate to the other end and thanked Nash with a smile as he moved the chair for her. Chapel went on talking as the hatch opened and the plump arms busied themselves. "And how long are you here for?"

"I don't know," Pyne said. He moved the bottle of wine, in pretense of making room as Mrs. Chapel brought a serving dish from the hatch, and refilled his own glass.

"You don't know?" Chapel lived in a world where nothing was unknown.

"No, sir."

"Well, I hope you'll enjoy your stay. What have you got with you?"

"I'm sorry?"

"Missiles."

Pyne looked into the bland eyes behind the dark-framed glasses. Why was Chapel asking? The War Office had been explicit on this: "You can answer any questions the P.O., Tokariji, asks. He runs the island and we can't ship anything in there without his knowledge. Anything we don't want him to know, you won't know either."

"We've got seven missiles here, Dr. Chapel. Six Javelin 33s and a Triton."

The eyes lost their blandness.

"A Triton?"

Pyne watched him steadily. A crooked tie and crumpled trousers, chalk on the sleeves of the jacket—but the picture was false. Looking out from this guise of an untidy and absent-minded boffin were the eyes of a superlative brain, and now they were sharp with hostility.

"What are you doing here with a Triton?"

"Training."

It was all the War Office had told him. If he had his own ideas he wasn't telling anyone, even the P.O., Tokariji. His own ideas were classified.

"If I am correct," Chapel said lightly, "the Triton is an intercontinental ballistic missile of some four thousand miles' range."

"You are correct."

Major Nash had begun worrying. Pyne had drunk three whiskies and half a bottle of wine. He was far from getting tight; he could go through a whole bottle of Scotch at a sitting and not show it. But it made him difficult to handle if he were in any way opposed; and from Chapel's sudden attitude Pyne was now offered opposition of a high order. Nash watched them both. He was now quite unaware of Mrs. Chapel.

"And the Triton," said Chapel almost softly, "normally carries a thousand-megaton nuclear warhead, when armed."

"It does."

"I assume that yours is unarmed."

Pyne had the hint of a smile on his long mouth, the smile of a warrior scenting blood.

"We don't train with live rounds."

"I'm glad."

"And surely the Principal Officer, Tokariji, would be

asked first, if we wanted to set up a nuclear-armed weapon on terrain under his authority?"

Chapel leaned forward an inch. "I would so expect."

Nash was sweating under his elegant mess jacket. He wished they'd never come here tonight. A sudden movement on the other side of the dining hatch gave him a start. Mrs. Chapel got up. The dessert was served.

"It's blueberry pie," she said, and Nash wondered if her smile could be considered brave or if she simply didn't know how dangerous things had got. "The Americans send it to us often from Midway, and we send them cases of Gentleman's Relish."

"How nice," said Nash.

"It's neighborly, isn't it?"

"Oh, very."

"I do hope you like blueberry pie, Major."

"My favorite."

He doubted if he'd taste much of it because Chapel was reopening the offensive:

"As a thinking man, Colonel Pyne, you must deplore the fact that while science is peaceably reaching out to other worlds, it's also arming men to destroy our own."

Pyne finished the wine in his glass. "I am, thank God, a simple soldier, Dr. Chapel. I'd lose too much sleep as a thinking man. I'd have to ask myself so many awkward questions—why, for instance, we spend thousands of millions on space research and at the same time put a tin can on the chemist's counter for pennies to help cure cancer."

Somewhere a telephone rang. Mrs. Chapel left the table. Nash took a desperate spoonful of pie.

"Peaceful science," Chapel said carefully, "has just produced the laser ray, which we are shortly to use in space research. It's already proving valuable in cancer surgery. In contrast, the cure effected by destroying an entire hospital full of patients as an indirect result of nuclear bombardment would seem less elegant." He looked up.

"Peter Follett," said his wife. "I do hope you don't have to—"

He was already on his way to the telephone. She sat down awkwardly and Nash made a noise with his spoon. "Quite delicious," he said.

"I'm so glad. May I help you to some more?"

"I've overdone things already."

And Chapel was standing in the middle of the room, shapeless and somehow relieved. "You must excuse me—I'm needed at Instrumentation." He turned away, feeling his pockets. "It was so very good of you to come."

Nash had half-risen. Pyne stayed as he was, his forearm on the table, his fingers spinning the glass. The amber-colored eyes remained fixed on the distant door that Chapel had closed.

"He doesn't like arguing," Mrs. Chapel said, her smile a little nervous. She gazed attentively at Pyne, but he said nothing. He still watched the door. "I've never heard him so forthright, with a guest. I'm so sorry, Colonel."

Nash was getting something ready to say when Pyne swung his head and looked at her directly—"I like a man who comes out fighting and it's a pity we had to cut it short." He smiled at her suddenly with narrowed eyes. "And certainly he had a point there. While he's rummaging around in the stars I'm here with my powder barrel. Only wants a match." His fingers spun the glass faster and its rim rang against the flower bowl.

She said quickly: "I do hope you'll take some brandy?"

"Thank you."

There seemed, Nash thought, a bigness that came to Ken when he was drinking, bigness and not just size. His voice grew gradually lower, deeper, and each of his words had the murmur of the lion. Yet he wasn't a man to whom alcohol lent artificial strength; he had his own true strength and a cold sober courage when it was needed. Nash had seen it himself, and in Cyprus ten of the company had lived because of it.

But it wasn't needed now. The bell had sounded and Chapel had left the ring. There was only, Nash thought unhappily, this poor little bitch to be put at her ease if they could manage.

When they left the alcove he drew the armchairs nearer together without being asked, while she brought a tray of coffee and the plump girl cleared the table; there was even conversation of a sort for ten minutes, based on the "neighborliness" between Tokariji and Midway Island, seven hundred miles distant; and Pyne drank two brandies to their one, sitting at his ease now with one leg stretched out and the balloon glass held on a raised knee, his head forward and his amber eyes raised to watch Mrs. Chapel.

Nash decided that in another ten minutes he would make signals and persuade Ken to give the retreat; there'd be a stock of brandy at the civilian senior mess. He was forestalled by a good three minutes and it was Sergeant Lacey who was shown in.

To please the lady present he snapped up a brilliant salute and stood with his thumbs along the seams. Pyne returned the honor by getting up, carefully guarding his glass.

"What's on fire, Lacey?"

"Compliments of Mr. Stoner, sir—there's a signal just come in."

"What's it say?"

"Coded, sir."

Pyne's eyes flickered downward and after a pause of three seconds he swung his head to look at Nash.

"I'm sure Mrs. Chapel would excuse you, Robert, if you went and took care of it."

Nash got the surprise off his face, thanked Mrs. Chapel

for a delightful evening, and took up his cap. Lacey had the door open for him.

When it was closed, Pyne turned to see his hostess watching him, and suddenly realized that her quick shy smile had its purposes: she used it to change whatever expression she would otherwise be caught in.

"Perhaps I should go, too." He made the gesture of looking at his watch.

"Please stay," she said. The smile meant nothing, but her eyes seemed bright, perhaps in contrast to the tan of her skin. When he had sat down again she brought the brandy from the tray and knelt to fill his glass.

Chapter 7

The buildings and installations on Tokariji were disposed in two large groups. The living quarters, stores, cinema, post office, and dockside sheds formed a group inside the "butt" of the "revolver" whose shape the island had. The "trigger guard" was the harbor, which lay between this group and the more sporadic installations on the other side. These were the technical buildings—Control Center, Instrumentation, Telemetry, and the actual range-head gantries, launchers, and ancillaries.

The airstrip, running along the "barrel," passed within a hundred yards of the harbor, leaving only a narrow neck of terrain between the two main groups of buildings. Through this narrow section ran the single road connecting both areas, and all traffic on normal business had to pass this way. The entire technical staff lived east of the harbor and worked west of it.

Halfway along this stretch of road was the security officer, ideally placed. Nobody could easily go from the living quarters to the technical installations unobserved from the security office windows. If Hurst's predecessor had not put the office there, Hurst would have put it there himself.

He had a staff of two clerks, one of whom worked in a room at the post office a mile away. The other kept a collection of files and records in a hut near the dockside.

Neither was qualified to receive or transmit classified information of any kind. Neither visited the main security office except on special summons from Hurst; if he wanted information from file he visited his clerks. Thus he was alone in his observation post throughout the working day and often at night, with three telephones to link him with the main switchboard and each of his staff. If someone had likened him to a spider on a web he would probably have been pleased with such an image.

His policy was to sense every infinitesimal vibration in the web and to examine its source. He made it his business to inform himself as widely and as deeply as he could on every aspect in the life of Tokariji. He was therefore on duty at all times and in all places, even in his bed during the hour before sleep came. Routine and official information was dealt with in his office; it was done efficiently and without much interest: he was unmoved by matters known to other people. His more interesting information came to him in different places, and he kept it all secure in his mind. Very little of it was ever passed on to London or anywhere else; most was stored and revised and reexamined in the light of other facts. He was thus possessor of a kind of library of jigsaw puzzles, and most of the pieces were aspects of the personal lives of the people on Tokariji.

Some of them were aware of this and resented it. Hurst noted everything. He would note that a certain technician seemed to be hitting the bottle a bit in the junior mess, and would slip this piece into the relevant jigsaw, to reexamine the whole. He would note that a certain scientist was working later than usual at night, and alone, and would fit this fact into all the others. He missed nothing and discarded nothing, and was the least popular man on the island, and probably the best security officer the island would ever have.

The day after his interrogation of Colonel Pyne he shut

the door of his office and switched on the tape recorder. Every single word that was spoken in this office went automatically onto tape, and no one had ever seen the microphone. Sometimes he would take an indexed spool from the locked cupboard and play it back, maybe months after the original recording; and sometimes a missing piece of a jigsaw would be found and fitted in.

His memory was good but he used the tape because a security risk would sooner or later convict himself from his own mouth: and Hurst would have it on record.

He had spent part of the night worrying about the interrogation of Colonel Pyne. Action would have to be taken, but he was not sure how far to go. A playback would help him to decide. He listened to Pyne's voice, and to his own. As always, the intonation and the timbre of the voices were magnified by the tape, and Pyne's had a low resonance that on this occasion was probably the surface tone of hidden anger.

The early part of the interview was uninteresting, and Hurst spun the machine at fast speed for a few seconds, stopped it, and set it to playback.

". . . Way, instead of coming Cairo–Karachi–Singapore?"

"I can't say."

"Do you mean you 'can't' say?"

"We flew in the direction our pilot was ordered. I was a passenger."

"I see."

"Now I must leave you. If you've further questions, I suggest you contact the War Office."

"Just a minute."

"I'm sorry, but—"

"Just a minute, please. You say your unit has been sent here for 'training.' Did you say that?"

"Oh, come along . . . your memory's reliable, surely."

"Quite reliable. You said you were here for 'training.' Why couldn't you train in England?"

"The War Office will know. It may or may not tell you."

"You must have asked *yourself* why you've been sent ten thousand miles to the middle of the Pacific Ocean—for 'training'?"

"If you say so."

"And what answer occurred to you?"

"This is a poor interrogation, you know. Most of your questions take the form of suppositions. If you'll now forgive me—"

"This missile, now—the Triton. It's got a range of four thousand miles. That's quite a long way. But even from a point in the middle of the Pacific it could reach quite a few interesting places. I'll ask a direct question. Why do you think the War Office has given you an ICBM to 'train' with, at this particular point on the earth's surface?"

"I'd say it's all part of some diabolical plan to unnerve the Australians at this critical time when we're two hundred runs behind with only three wickets to go."

"Is it the first ICBM you've 'trained' with?" Hurst asked doggedly.

"Let me put you out of your misery before I go. We have a Triton here with us as part of the Alliance Program and we are ordered to practice handling, aiming, and firing techniques. We shall not in fact be firing it, nor has it a warhead. A Triton, fired without a warhead, is fully capable of knocking down a dog kennel. Our orders to refrain from firing were given as a result of pressure from the Canine Defense League. I'll say good morning."

The sound of quick footsteps.

"Do you decline to answer my questions?"

Pyne's voice was fainter.

"No. I refuse. You are not empowered to ask any member of the armed services in uniform any questions beyond those relevant to his credentials, which you have already put to me and I've already answered most readily."

The sound of the door opening.

"Will you please repeat the gist of that—you refuse to answer further questions?"

"Certainly. I refuse."

Footsteps again, growing fainter.

Hurst stopped the machine and stood looking down at it. How much had he learned? Nothing about the true functions of Pyne's unit. Nothing about the true reasons for the unit's having been sent here westward via Midway. But a lot had been learned about Pyne, the man; and this much evidence of his character could have been obtained only by provoking him. Action would of course have to be taken, but it didn't look as if there was much here for London.

He cut the section from the tape, spun it onto a miniature filing spool, and stored it in the cupboard under the new 387, the code number for Colonel Pyne. Action had been taken. Its effect might be produced within a week or a month or much longer than that, according to the shape of the other pieces that would be collected for this new jigsaw.

One question remained. Had this man been provoked easily because he was psychologically "interrogation-resistant" (a common case)? Or because he had known that these particular questions were not officially permissible? Or because he *did* know why his unit had been ordered ten thousand miles from home to "train" with an ICBM they would "not in fact be firing"?

Before locking the cupboard Hurst stood for a moment with his pale red-rimmed eyes on the hundreds of miniature spools, an archive of statements and admissions—some, as he knew, made incautiously as the result of his careful provocation—of which he was the secret custodian. For this little moment he gazed engrossed, like a miser counting his gold.

"Well, we shan't finish tonight and that's a fact!"

"There's tomorrow, isn't there?"

"Third bloody day at it! Ask me, Ken's gone off his bloody loaf."

"He knows what he's doing."

"Tell you what he's not bloody doing—he's not workin' his bloody guts to the marrow, like we are. You know how far we are from the Equator? You c'd spit there, with your mouth shut!"

"You'd sprain something if you tried to get that shut."

"Listen! Couple of hours with that high-clearance loader an' we'd've got the job done with, bloody yesterd'y!"

"Well it's a civvy loader and we're in the peaceful service of the Queen. Work it out for yourself."

"But Jesus Christ, this whole bloody pit was dug out by civvies!"

"Shame they didn't drop you in it and sprinkle the earth, then. I'd've said the amen."

On the third day the planks were lined up and the main body of the Triton was hauled over them on the jacking trolley, and the gantry received it. There had been no damage.

"Decent enough operation," Nash said.

"Not irregular."

Pyne had stood for the last hour watching the missile gantried. Twice Nash had come up to speak to him, but there was a mood on Ken that he didn't fathom. It was as if Ken had got the thing there all by himself.

This mood had been triggered off three days ago when Stoner had reported the terrain too rough for normal transport. He had told his C.O. that the civilian authority had a high-clearance loader that would do the job, and Ken had rounded on him—"Since when has the army been dependent on civilian assistance?"

Stoner had asked Nash later: "Well, what the hell did I say that was wrong?"

"Nothing. Better just not say it again is all I know."

Three days' work had been ordered, the whole unit slogging in the heat of the sun with plank gear and cable, practically manhandling the main body from the dockside to the weapon pit.

Of course Nash knew it was to do with that freak Chapel opening a gratuitous offensive against Ken, who was meant to be a guest at the dinner table. The unit had never been too proud to ask for civilian help in the normal course of events, nor too stuffy to give the civilians a hand if extra man power could win the day on a tricky job. Ken was now making it clear that henceforth a civilian was lower than a louse.

Nash worried about this for two reasons. One was that Ken didn't easily bear a grudge, yet this mood of his had lasted three days already and he was damned tricky to approach. The other thing was that it was going to be difficult for the whole unit to live out their tour of duty on Tokariji if the C.O. were at odds with the civilians who ran the place.

"All tied up," he said, trying to sound cheerful. The men were coming away from the gantry and Stoner was checking the rig. Sergeant-major Rice was sweating like a pig; they all were, come to that. "Two rounds of free beer tonight, Ken?"

For a minute Nash thought the question hadn't been heard. The C.O. stood motionless, staring across at the missile in the gantry. Then he said without turning his head: "They've all worked very well under trying conditions. I venture to hope that their satisfaction in a job well done will offer sufficient reward."

"Yes, sir."

Nash left him, ostensibly going down into the weapon pit

to watch Captain Stoner check the rig. His relations with Ken were pretty good and of more than a few years' standing, but if ever he'd come close to disliking him it was when he talked like a pinstripe-trousered bumped-up bloody politician.

Stoner was tapping the turnbuckles and Nash asked him: "All okay?"

"Spot-on." Stoner gazed down at him. "Don't look so worried, we didn't bust anything." He wiped the sweat from his neck with a sodden handkerchief.

"I'm not worried."

It was too easy to pin Ken's mood on just that one brush with the enemy. (That was how Ken himself would put it—"the enemy.") Then what could it be damned well pinned on? Who else, apart from Chapel, could have riled the man? No one in the unit. Griggs, the civilian administrator here, couldn't have given them a better welcome. They were the only people they'd set eyes on, except for Chapel's wife.

Stoner came down from the gantry apron. "That's it, then. The boys've done their nut on this baby—how about telling Ken they've earned a beer ration?"

Nash looked away. "I don't think we ought to spoil them."

"We could ask him, anyway."

"As his representative," said Nash, "I've good reason to believe I'm expressing what would be his own opinion." He walked away, angry with Stoner, Ken, and himself. Who was talking like a bumped-up politician now?

A stray thought was tugging at him: Chapel's wife. She was the only person they'd had any contact with, apart from Griggs and Chapel himself. It wasn't likely that she had anything to do with Ken's mood; yet it had been a bit of a facer when Ken had sent him off like that to look after the coded signal. The poor little bitch had bored him rigid and he'd shown as much. Why had he decided to stay there, alone with her? She wasn't his type.

He worried the thing, climbing the iron ladder from the weapon pit. The C.O. was the only one in the whole unit who had the key to the special-duties code; he'd known his adjutant couldn't "go and take care of it" when he'd sent him away that night. Stoner had been the duty officer and he'd sent Lacey, the duty N.C.O., with the message to say that a signal had come through. All Nash had been able to do was join Stoner in the signals office and report that the C.O. would be along. It was an hour before Ken had come; he had read the signal and simply told the clerk to lock it away and send a coded reply; then he had turned in without a word to Nash.

He climbed from the shadow of the pit into the light of the lowering sun. Outlines were edged with gold—the humped shapes of the Nissen huts, the blocky square of the signals office, the trellis of the radio mast, which reared not far from the pit. Ken had gone. Someone was moving away along the ridge left by the excavations, a civilian in a dark shirt. He was out of bounds here, within a hundred yards of the missile installation, and ought to be told.

On second thoughts, civilians were best left alone. What, then, had been in that damned signal? Why hadn't the C.O. mentioned it to his own adjutant?

It was too easy to pin Ken's mood on just that one brush with Chapel. Tackle him? No future there. Stick it out and hope for better things tomorrow.

It was quiet in the senior mess, even at the bar. One of the civilians had offered Captain Stoner a beer and he knocked it off within a minute. He'd been dreaming of that beer all day.

The civilian was perched on the barstool like a plump robin, watching the few people here.

"Is it normally as quiet as this?" Stoner asked him.

The man turned his pale eyes on him. "Not normally.

They've got a new project in—the White Lance. It's never been flight-tested, so it's rather an unknown quantity." He flattened his lips into a bright smile. "Don't worry, it's non-classified. Have another."

"My round."

"I'm all behind. Go on, have another—you've earned it, I know that." He spoke to the barman and gazed at the officer again with his slightly red-rimmed eyes. "I was watching you chaps at it, like ants with a sugar lump. A soldier's life is no sinecure, I can see that. Why didn't you borrow the high-clearance loader?"

"God knows. I suggested it, but our C.O. wouldn't play."

"Well, that's funny. You could've done the job a lot quicker, with that. Your C.O. sounds a bit dim, if you don't mind me saying so."

Stoner sat an inch straighter and put some money down for the barman.

"That's on me," the civilian said.

"Good of you, but I'd rather do it."

He took the beer and the change.

"After all," the plump man said, choosing simple words as if explaining something to a child, "you people are here in a place run by civilians—you're guests here, call it that. So if you want any help, you've only got to ask." His bright smile was rather pointless, Stoner thought. "Surely your C.O. hasn't got anything against harmless civilians? He was invited over to the principal officer's own house the other night, I know that."

Captain Stoner spoke studiously into midair. "It's just that our C.O. is the type who prefers doing things without anyone's help, civilian or otherwise. Not a bad fault in a commanding officer." He looked directly at the plump man. "Are you a scientist?"

"Me? Oh, I'm not anybody."

"I thought I'd seen you around."

"I'm not surprised. I get about a bit."

Stoner nodded, put some money down for the barman and told him: "A beer for my good friend." He then excused himself under polite protest.

He was met by Major Nash on his way out of the mess. Nash said: "I wondered where you'd got to."

"I'm off duty."

"I didn't mean that. Have you seen Wilson?"

Nash still had that worried look. All in all, thought Stoner, there wasn't anyone on this bloody island he wasn't rapidly getting fed up with.

"The last I saw of him, he was trying to organize a billiard table for the boys."

"See if you can find him," Nash said. "We're reporting to the C.O. at 19.00 hours—that's in ten minutes' time."

"What's happened now?"

"It's all I know."

Chapter 8

Eve had seen the light go out in his office, across in the Instrumentation Building; its reflection was gone from the harbor. By the time the door sounded, below in the house, she had put on a blue nightgown and stood in front of the mirror, trying to see herself as he would see her.

It said in the chapter about the sexual responsibility of the wife that excessive modesty was a barrier to harmonious marriage relations, and that the normal husband took a natural pleasure in seeing the lightly clad body of his partner, when the occasion was opportune.

"You're no pinup," she murmured to her reflection. "Too thin." The sound of her own voice embarrassed her and she turned away. His keys jingled on the stairs. He always brought them up with him and put them on the shelf by his bed, last thing, with his wristwatch. The only other person with keys to his office was Mary. Keys were important on Tokariji. She hated them.

"Hello, Jim."

She got to the dressing table just in time and was doing her hair when he came in. If she didn't make an attractive picture it was the best she knew how to do.

"Aren't you cold?" he asked, and in a flash she told herself it was his kindness.

"I'm warm," she said. "Come and feel."

He hung up his jacket and pulled at his laces. "They told me the crate had shifted, so I went down to look. On first inspection there's no damage."

"You mustn't look for trouble already, Jim."

"With this one we can't leave anything to chance."

"You never do, with any of them." She watched him go into the bathroom and when the door was shut she looked at her face in the mirror and softly smiled, to hide any other expression. Beside her head, reflected in the glass, was a small ruby glow in the window, and she went across to it. They were the three lamps at the top of the radio mast, not far from where the colonel lived with his men.

She was standing there, her feet bare on the warm pine floor and the hairbrush still in her hand, when Jim came out of the bathroom in his black silk dressing gown. It had been a present from her; she had thought he would look dramatic in it; but it didn't really suit him. He looked wrong in it, as if he were dressing up as a mandarin. It was kind of him to go on wearing it.

"People can see you," he said.

She drew the curtains across. "Would anyone bother to look?"

It didn't necessarily mean, the chapter on responsibility said, that a wife had simply to disrobe, or partly disrobe, before her partner, in order to bring about his desired approach. The normal husband had much on his mind, especially after his day's work.

"In twelve years, Jim, I haven't put on an inch any-where." She looked down at herself, slowly lifting her bare arms. "Good marks?"

"You'll never change," he said, and took off his watch, to put it on the shelf by his bed with the keys. "You'll always be my Eve."

The scent of toothpaste was on the air; it was the smell of reading time. He switched on the lamp above his bed and took out the bookmark, propping the book against his knees, which were raised under the bedclothes.

The night was so still that as she stood there she could detect the sound of the nylon brushing across her nipples as she breathed. He had, she thought, a nice face, with kindness in it, and intelligence; those eyes had never in all the years regarded hers with less than goodwill in them. Few women could say that.

Timber creaked somewhere in the house, contracting as the night brought coolness; it was the sound of lying awake, of loneliness.

Suddenly she felt as she had only once felt before, with him, in all that time; not quite anger but more than protest.

"I apologized to Colonel Pyne for you," she said. "I thought you'd want me to."

She moved to the dressing table and put the brush down; it looked rather useless lying there.

"Pyne?"

She said: "You thought he was swanking, about his missile, I expect. You didn't mean to get at him like that. He said he liked a good argument and was sorry you had to leave us."

Crossing the room to her bed, she felt naked; it wasn't the time now to show what little she had in the way of charm—the book would have told her that.

"You didn't tell me until the last minute that we were having him to dinner, Eve. Of course you meant well, but I would really prefer to make my own apologies when there's any occasion for it."

That was his answer, she knew; there'd be nothing more said unless she made a point of it.

"You look so cold," he added.

"Blue is a cold color." She didn't prop her pillow up or reach for her novel. "I'm sorry you don't like him."

"Do you want to talk about it?"

"Yes." Her own answer surprised her.

There was a little pause. He never replied to anything important immediately.

"The presence of an army unit on Tokariji disturbs me," he said carefully. "I'd been told it was coming, of course; in fact I had to be consulted. Finding myself face to face with an army officer at my own table rather brought home to me what I'd permitted on paper. So be it. My aversion to war and everything to do with war is not any fault in Pyne. But I think, yes, that he made a point of showing himself pleased to be in charge of a most hideous weapon. Even the least imaginative soldier should be expected to feel some kind of awareness when he's training with a missile capable of destroying a whole city at a blow. Pyne seemed rather proud of it."

"But, Jim, it hasn't got a warhead. He said so."

"No. But the Triton can be fitted with a nuclear warhead, aimed, triggered, and fired within twenty-three minutes. He and his men are training to complete that final operation inside that time limit, using at the moment a dummy nose cone. The crew of the airplane that destroyed Hiroshima made thirty training runs over a simulated target area, carrying a dummy bomb. We were then at war and we are now at peace, however delicate the balance. It seems that the East and West can live in compromise, as far as Russia is concerned. Communist China is more sparing with her assurances and she's already tested her first nuclear weapon. I'm sorry, but in the light of these facts I find Colonel Pyne's attitude appallingly casual."

She lay on her side, leaning on her elbow so as to face him. Did he know that with a word she could hurt him deeply? Yes, he knew; and he believed she didn't want to hurt him; and he was right.

It had never been mentioned between them since he had confessed it to her soon after they had met. He had told her

67

that when he was twenty-four years old—"old enough to know right from wrong," as he put it—he had worked on the final trigger stages of the first atomic bomb, and was therefore partly responsible for "the first sin that science had ever known." She had said: "If you hadn't done that particular work, someone else would have." He had answered: "Yes. But it was me."

In the year following Hiroshima he had spent two months in the psychiatric ward of St. Helen's, as a result of "overwork." Since that year his friends had told her that he had changed, and one of them advised her against the marriage. "Old Chapel"—still only twenty-nine at that time—was said to be "unstable."

Perhaps it was partly to prove them wrong that she had married him; it was in her nature to fly against forebodings of any kind. Then they had said that she hadn't proved them wrong but that her influence on him had steadied him; and they praised her for it. And she knew that they were wrong again.

She was surprised when he spoke again. He had not gone back to his reading, but was still watching her, his eyes troubled. "There's something else, Eve, that has occupied my mind lately."

Her thoughts flew to the sandy cove and the rock and she realized suddenly that she felt guilty and wondered why.

"Yes, Jim?"

He could never have seen her down there.

In the stillness she felt the beat of her heart vibrating the spring mattress.

"Just before Pyne's unit arrived I was given a report from the main radar post. They had sighted a high-altitude reconnaissance aircraft over the island. We have never seen one before. I decided it was possible that the digging of the Army weapon pit had excited interest, and that information about it was being passed out of Tokariji—unwittingly, of course. I asked Mr. Hurst what he thought, and he told me he'd occupy himself with it, unofficially. Again, this is no fault of Colonel Pyne, but the idea that his coming here might have brought foreign surveillance on my establishment doesn't endear him to me."

She didn't want to talk any more, even about this new thing; she didn't want to listen any more to his tidy and reasonable arguments.

"Everything will be all right, Jim. It always is, with you."

"It always has been," he said, "since you came." And then as if he were afraid of having exposed himself too much he said: "Aren't you reading tonight?"

She hadn't switched on the lamp above her bed.

"No." She drew up the sheet and smiled for him, watched him go back to his book, reading to herself its title, sideways, her head on the pillow. It was *An Analysis of Exchange Processes in Thermodynamics*. What was it like, she wondered, to be able to understand even the title of a book like that one?

She murmured, "I heard what you said, Jim, and I thank you," but he did not hear.

Long after he had put the light out she lay with her eyes not quite closed, watching the glow in the window where the curtains left a gap; she had never noticed before how the lamps on the radio mast shone into this room, all night. From secret places in the house the cooling timber creaked; it was lying awake time, and she lay with her arm between her legs, watching the window.

On June 4, the day after the *Maid of Mersey* reached port at Tokariji with her cargo, Dr. Chapel paused on his way through to his office and told Mary:

"Now we can talk about it."

He stood with his hands fumbling in the pockets of his

jacket, looking a little lost, as if he needed her help. She knew in a way that he did.

This day would go into the records as Day 1, Phase 1. It was the first day of the first phase in the preparation of the new experiment, White Lance. The mood of the P.O. was on every scientist and technician on the island, and it was known among them as "new-shoot nerves." The strangest thing about this mood was that for the next two months it would get worse instead of better. The new vehicle had arrived, and nobody would be at peace again until it had reached nine hundred miles into the magnetosphere on the first, last, and only flight of its life.

"It'll be a relief, Dr. Chapel," she said.

But there was a difference about today's mood. White Lance would be the first of its kind to be fired; it was the most powerful that Tokariji had been asked to handle; and its performance was to a great extent unpredictable. Further, there had been no period of relaxation between the last shoot and this one; the disaster to BJ-9 hung over them still, even though its cause had been found, even though everyone here had been cleared of responsibility.

Yesterday Alec Griggs of administration had told her: "Tomorrow's going to be a day and a half. How are you feeling?"

"I shan't be having anything to do with White Lance."

"Tell the Marines. You'll be nursing the P.O. through the whole schedule, day in and day out. There's only one nightmare I'd run from quicker than handling this shoot and that's handling Jim."

"He'll be all right."

Alec had answered quietly: "Then everything will."

She looked now at the man in the shapeless clothes, and thought of the size of the WL-1 experiment, and felt fear for him, and knew he felt none for himself.

"We shall have a good time, Mary. We shall all have a

very good time." The reflection of early sunlight in the windows shone across his glasses and she couldn't see his eyes; but he was smiling.

She said: "The best we have ever had." And he went through into his office and she thought: *It's begun*.

From the windows of the Instrumentation Building it looked like a state funeral.

The trailer was eighty feet long and it moved at slower than walking pace, bearing the single crate from the dockside to the Technical Area. On each side walked men, and others hemmed the route. People had come across from the living quarters—people who knew no more of a rocket than that it went up into the air, the wives of technicians, the canteen staffs, cleaners, storekeepers, post-office clerks, and laundry girls—and they lined the route to watch White Lance go by.

They saw nothing but the long rough-wood crate; all they knew of the rocket was that it was long, very long. And that it was here.

Among the men who paced beside the trailer were six armed guards; they had come the whole way from Liverpool and now walked with their coats off in the heat of the sun. With them walked security officers, and Hurst was talking to them, asking them questions.

The trailer was taking very little weight. The rocket was empty of fuel and its ancillaries were being transported separately in trucks and loaders. White Lance was lying down, a seventy-foot length of thin metal skin cradled in antishock clamps to safeguard against movement. There must be no jolting; the metal skin was so thin that a man could kick a hole in it; later, when the fuel was pumped in under pressure, White Lance would become strong enough to stand upright.

Near the head of the transporter walked a group of scientists; they had no purpose here; there was nothing for

71

them to do; there was simply nowhere else they wished to be. They were the specialist team who had come to Tokariji weeks before to await the rocket; they would be here to see it grow and to see it die. Among them were P. K. S. Whymlett, Officer in Scientific Charge, a big man who walked with little steps; the others were the missile project chief, the trials superintendent, and the senior representatives of the Wymark-Vincent group, who had built White Lance.

For different men, WL-1 had different meanings: it was a project or an experiment, an instrument for measuring stratospheric conditions or for the exploration of the unknown, a test platform for electronic installations that were themselves on trial, or simply a technical unit designed to perform in ways required of it; but for all of them it represented the needs deepest in them: the need to foster and to love a thing that they had made themselves, and the need to hear men say that the thing they had made was good.

One man walked by himself, his hands behind his back, and sometimes stopped and stood at a little distance so that he could take in the whole scene. He watched the turning of the trailer's thirty wheels, and the route ahead, and the lie of the long crate and the tension of the cables that held it steady. He was responsible, as ground safety officer, for the life and well-being of every man who worked on WL-1 from this day onward. He watched for a spark or a snapping rope or a coatsleeve dangling near the trailer wheels; later he would watch for a leaking pressure gauge or a loose connection or the signs of fatigue in a technician.

Behind the trailer moved a group of officers on their way to the range head. They were the chiefs of Missile Acceptance, Launching, Trials Control, Experimentation, Ground Command, and Area Operations. On this day each of them had become as much a component of WL-1 as the autopilot unit or the gyro system of the rocket itself; their minds and hands would be linked with the intricate circuits of White Lance until, in two months' time, it broke free of earth.

Before noon the trailer reached No. 1 Test Shop, across from the Instrumentation Building, and from the flat roof a score of people watched for twenty minutes as the long crate was maneuvered between the doors and positioned precisely below the hydraulic slings. The engine of the trailer horse was switched off, and for a little time there was silence but for the hum of the dust extractor plant. No one spoke; there was nothing, really, to say.

Then the tall doors were rolled together and the men broke up and moved away; and some among those who watched from the roof of the Instrumentation Building had the odd illusion of seeing the beginning of an execution, with its trappings of deliberation and solemnity. White Lance, born in the design studios more than four years ago in England, had been brought here to be destroyed.

Chapter 9

At 11.00 hours on June 5 Colonel Pyne ordered a detachment group of twelve men with officers and N.C.O.s to report to the airstrip control tower. He himself arrived ten minutes later with his adjutant and Lieutenant Wilson.

Major Nash, Captain Stoner, and Lieutenant Wilson were the only members of the group who knew what was on. On the evening of their abrupt summons to the C.O.'s room, Colonel Pyne had told them:

"In two days' time there's an aircraft of Air Transport Command landing here and we are to receive its freight with urgent precautionary drill."

Some of Nash's despondency was lifted. This must be the subject of the coded signal, and it might be simply that Ken's difficult mood was nothing more than natural apprehension. Once this freight was received safely he'd return to his old self.

"The consignment is a solid-fuel motor still on the secret list and we may expect subsequent orders to install it in the Triton. Until such orders arrive we are to store it in the concrete blockhouse below the north rim of the weapon pit and mount a constant guard of two men and a junior N.C.O. My special orders about this will be posted at 12.00 hours on June 5. Meanwhile, Stoner, you can inform

Sergeant-major Rice that such duties are imminent, so that he can work out the roster."

"Right, sir."

Nash asked: "What's the thing called?"

"I have not finished."

They stiffened, every face was expressionless. Nash thought: Christ, it's like being back at Sandhurst.

"As you know, urgent precautionary drill with any solid-fuel motor is on standing orders. In this case you are to ensure that at no time—at no time—will there be the slightest instance of failure to comply with this drill. Any form of negligence, however trivial, will be reported to me personally and at once. My orders are to impress this on you with all force."

He turned away and stood at the open window, looking up at the lamps on the radio mast, hands clasped behind him, a finger fretting against the thumb.

Nash felt Stoner glance at him but didn't turn his head. Someone swallowed and they all heard it in the quiet room.

The C.O. was suddenly facing them again and saying in a lower tone: "In my unit, as in all other units of the British Services, there are sometimes occasions when trivial breaches of discipline are deliberately overlooked. Without a few degrees of human tolerance no army can hold together, particularly in peacetime. But there are instances where even the slightest breach of discipline can have very grave consequences, and this is such an instance. Bear it well in mind. The safety of every one of us on this island—and I include the civilian establishment—depends on the discipline we shall enforce with reference to the handling and guarding of this component."

The amber eyes reviewed their faces. They stood gazing the regulation few inches above his head.

"So far as I know, this 'thing' hasn't a name. The serial

classification letters happen to be CHL-stroke-one. All right, somebody name the baby."

The whole unit was used to the C.O.'s sudden change of manner when he wished it to be known that business was over and they were off parade; but his earlier attitude had been so uncompromising that it was a second or two before the first of them—Stoner—looked down and said:

"Charlie."

"Couldn't miss, at that range. Charlie it is. Now let's have a cigarette."

Now they stood waiting on the apron outside the airstrip control tower, watching the sky. Sergeant Lacey had brought the medium loader along from the M. T. Section and there were twelve men for handling.

At 11.30 they heard the sound of the aircraft and C.S.M. Rice called them together. "You know the orders. You've been long enough in a missile unit to know what's meant by 'urgent precautionary drill.'" He judged the C.O. to be out of earshot and thus felt free to deliver his homily in a manner that would leave nothing to doubt. "So just get it straight. This lot's dynamite, and the first one of you to drop so much as a fart is going to blow this whole bloody island out of the sea, so for God's sake, keep a grip on your rings."

Major Nash had never known anything like it. The unit had worked together for years, most of the time under their present C.O. As a missile group they had often handled dangerous weaponry, and there'd never been any trouble. Today it was murder.

Colonel Pyne was present when the crated motor and separately packed ancillaries were taken off the medium loader and stored in the concrete blockhouse. The rest of the unit, not operationally involved, lined the rim of the weapon pit to have a look. But there was utter silence as the work went on, except for an occasional order.

It was not, thought Nash, the presence of a new and apparently dangerous component that caused this hush; it was the presence of the C.O. His recent soreheadedness had affected the whole unit, and everyone was edgy when he was anywhere near.

Pyne stood not far from the doorway of the blockhouse, feet astride and hands tucked behind. The men's shadows were sharp-etched and dumpy under the fierce noon sun.

"Sar'nt Lacey!"

"Sir?"

"Get that banding grounded."

"Sir!"

They worked with ten-inch eagle wrenches but wielded them tenderly, as if everything they touched were made of glass. It took half an hour to get the main component uncrated and shipped in the lugs ready for storing, and the men on the rim of the pit bent forward, staring down. So this was "Charlie." Not much to look at. But they went on looking at it. The main jacket was painted with stove-black and had three bright orange rings. A couple of positioning guides and that was all. But you had to go on looking at it. The thing was so black, in the bright sun, like a lump of night.

"Mr. Stoner!"

"Yes, sir?"

"Keep those two men clear of the doorway and rig your tackle higher. Risk of static."

"Right, sir."

One of the N.C.O.s dropped a lever and swore, jumping out of his skin; its metal rang like an alarm bell; he jerked a look at the C.O.'s face and wished he hadn't.

"Parks! Get the sweat off your hands!"

"Yes, Sarge."

They were passing a towel between them. The sun was in the pit with them and they fried.

A man murmured: "Do with a bloody drink, Dave, eh?"

"Shuddup, you silly sod. He'll have your guts out."

"Brown! Cut out that talking!"

"Yes, Sergeant."

They worked uneasily and Nash thought: this is dangerous. The C.O. had them in such a state of nerves that they couldn't control their movements properly. Accidents happened that way.

Wires ran from the components to the ground; from every tool and from every piece of metal they touched, wires ran to the ground because of the risk of a spark. They worked entangled.

"Mr. Wilson—straighten up that rail."

"There's a bolt to go in before we—"

"*Straighten it up!*"

They worked with the sweat dripping from their chins. At 13.20 hours the night-black component was ushered into the dark oblong of the doorway, and the sun's light was innocent again.

"Mount the guard, Sar'nt-major."

"Sir!"

The corporal and two men were standing by, and froze to attention. The rest of the men moved away from the blockhouse, at a loss to know whether they were dismissed or whether Ken was going to give them another tousing. The officers stood at ease, awaiting orders.

Pyne said nothing but turned away and came face to face with Hurst.

Nash, watching the C.O. in case there were to be an order, saw the expression on his face as he recognized the security man.

Quickly and quietly Nash said: "Sar'nt-major, dismiss working party."

Pyne had stopped, and stood with his feet together, looking at Hurst. They were right in the center of the weapon pit, and the men lining the rim above the blockhouse saw the C.O.'s attitude. They knew him well; they knew the set of his cap and the angle of his shoulders; they knew the stance of his legs and the knot of his folded hands; and they knew the significance of all the little differences in his aspect from day to day; and one man, watching from above the arena, muttered for the benefit of his companions: "If I was you, mate, I'd run." It was of course addressed, however inaudibly, to Hurst.

Pyne spoke and his voice had the timbre of a muffled drum. "What are you doing here?"

"Just checking up." Hurst gave a bright smile.

Sergeant-major Rice had dismissed the working party and they were moving away from the blockhouse almost on tiptoe, keeping their distance from the two men.

"Mr. Hurst." His tone was so low that it would have been heard only by the civilian, on open ground; but the walls of the pit trapped every word. "This area is strictly out of bounds to civilian personnel of whatever category. You will be good enough to leave."

The flat bright smile remained fixed, but color was mounting on the security man's neck. "You put her to bed nicely. Neat handling. I have to check up, you see. That's my job. Security. It's on the secret list, did you know?"

The heat struck down into the pit. Nowhere did any man move. C.S.M. Rice gave up the idea of trying to shepherd his flock toward the ladder and stood to a kind of desperate attention.

The cap tilted upward an inch.

"As the commander of this area on conditions of active service I am empowered to request you to leave. In the event of your noncompliance with that request I am empowered to order the use of force. Do you intend to comply with my request?"

Hurst slowly folded his arms. The flush had spread from his neck to his face.

It didn't matter, thought Major Nash, that the odds against the civilian were unfair. Hurst was alone among thirty hostile men, because—strangely enough—the whole unit was suddenly a hundred per cent on the side of their commanding officer. Whether they knew it or not, Hurst had become a kicking-boy for them. The C.O. had been looking for someone to kick, the last few days, and no one in the unit had given him any excuse. Now there was this fat little civvy buzzing about on their own ground as if he owned the place, and they looked forward to seeing him kicked into Christendom. This didn't matter, Nash thought, because Ken would treat the man just the same if there were only the two of them to fight it out; it wasn't Ken's fault that Hurst had poked his nose in at a time when the whole unit was looking on. What did matter was that Ken was going to stick his neck out on principle, simply because he'd been caught in the right mood to do it. That could be dangerous. There was more here than an army officer facing a security man; the Ministry of Defense was about to kick the Ministry of Information in the pants, and God knew what would happen when London heard of it. By Hurst's attitude, London would certainly hear.

Despite the flush on his face his voice was perfectly steady. "Anything that happens on this island affects security. You see, it's bound to, isn't it? And it's my job to check up—it doesn't matter what it is. I think the little mistake you're inclined to make is that just because you've got a brass insignia on your shirt you can do whatever you like." His bright smile appeared, and Nash, standing not far from the two men, looked away. A bright smile, worn on a face suffused with anger, was like a paper hat stuck on the head of a maddened bull. "I can quite see," Hurst went on, "that anyone who spends long enough trotting up and down in uniform begins thinking he can boss whoever he likes, civilians included. But you can't, you see. And I think it's time you knew."

Captain Stoner was weighing things up in his philosophical way. The lid was going to come off this lot, because neither man was prepared to lose face now. When Whitehall had read all the reports, would Ken be replaced or would the whole unit be slung out of Tokariji? The latter was preferable. Ken was normally a good type to soldier with and it'd be a pity to lose him, whereas there were plenty of better places the unit could be sent to than this crumby rock.

He heard Ken's patience breaking.

"You are requested to leave. Do you intend to comply?"

"No. You see, I don't have to, and—"

"*Sar'-major!*"

"Sir?"

"Muster two men as escort—at the double!"

"Sir!" C.S.M. Rice spun about. "Thompson! Brock!"

The C.O. was now at attention. "The civilian will be escorted to the boundary. Any resistance will be overcome by force."

As the two men positioned themselves one on each side of him, Hurst said: "Enjoy yourself. You won't be here very long."

"Escort will proceed!"

It took the three of them half a minute to reach the steel ladder. During this time there was no sound but their footsteps. A private climbed first; the civilian followed; the other private climbed last.

Then on the rim of the weapon pit a man laughed suddenly and others took it up until the C.S.M. cut them down with a look.

Colonel Pyne ordered all ranks to dismiss. Rice got his party out at a quick march and not one man broke step. The officers followed, their gait exemplary.

The guard stood fast at the blockhouse. Unmindful of them, Pyne remained standing in the center of the pit, alone.

Chapter 10

"Well, what are we going to do about him?" asked Captain Stoner.

"Nothing." Major Nash ordered another round. His limit was two doubles. Tonight he was going to make it three. "Sweat it out."

"But the boys are getting worried." He moved to give some room to a couple of civilians. The bar was doing good business tonight; a crowd of boffins had just come in, yammering away about the new missile they were setting up.

"Then the boys'll have to sweat it out, too," Nash said. "They know Ken's all right. Give him a bit of peace and he'll come up smiling."

"If you ask me, he's spoiling for a bit of a war." He finished his drink and picked up the one Nash had got for him. "I suppose it's not woman trouble again?"

Nash said: "I really don't feel it's our place to discuss the C.O.'s private affairs."

"Oh Lord, don't you start, Bob."

Nash put some more soda in his glass. This was the third and he'd have to make it last. "Did that sound starchy?"

"Just at the edges."

"I didn't mean it that way. Trouble is that as the adjutant of a unit that's been on bloody good terms with itself for a longish time I find I'm on the wrong foot now there's a bit of trouble. And don't forget that it's thanks to Ken that trouble's a rarity."

"And also that you're on the wrong foot now."

"Well, it's my foot so it's probably my fault. If you want to do anything about anybody, do it about me."

Stoner said equably, "I know just the thing." He tried to signal the barman.

Nash stopped him with a reluctant grin. "I'm over my limit, but you help yourself."

Stoner stopped signaling. "I suppose I spoke out of turn anyway. You're quite right. If you can't handle Ken, no one can. We'll all leave it to you." He finished his drink. "I'm going to see if the boys'll give me a game. Frank finally organized a billiard table. You staying here?"

"For a bit."

Nash was glad when he went. He didn't want to talk any more about Ken; nor did he want to be told that the whole unit would leave it up to him to stop the rot that was setting in. Ken wasn't a man you could fully reach, at the best of times; there was an inner defense you came up against and could never break. The junior officers addressed their adjutant, informally, as Bob; his C.O. called him Robert. Well, that was maybe a good thing; discipline depended a great deal on formality.

But it didn't make things any easier to deal with.

"Good evening, Major Nash."

That meant another drink. Well, what the hell.

He asked: "May I offer you something?"

"No, thank you." Her quick shy smile refreshed him. "Am I disturbing you?"

"Of course not." She was wearing a blue sailcloth thing, tunic and slacks, and he liked her in it. "You look marvelous." He supposed he shouldn't have said that. *In vino*, and so forth. Never mind.

"Thank you," she said. "I oughtn't to wear slacks in the mess but I've just finished helping them in the canteen."

"Everyone ought to wear slacks in the mess." Come to think of it, ninety per cent of the people in here were men.

She said: "Will you tell me what happened today?"

"Happened?"

"About Colonel Pyne and Mr. Hurst."

He took a quick look around. "Well, nothing much." He was suddenly stone cold sober.

"I've heard various reports," she said with quaint seriousness, "but you were actually there."

"Yes, well, Hurst came loafing about in the weapon pit, and Ken asked him to leave, and he wouldn't—"

"Ken is Colonel Pyne?"

"Sorry—Colonel Pyne, yes—"

"Go on calling him Ken."

"Oh. Right. Well, Hurst wouldn't leave, so Ken had him escorted back in bounds. That's all."

"And who was right?"

Rather too stiffly he said: "Ken, of course."

She was smiling impishly now. "You mean Mr. Hurst was actually sort of marched off the premises?"

"Yes. Won't you have a ginger ale, even?"

"All right. Then you can go on drinking."

Dammit, surely it wasn't showing. She couldn't have meant it that way.

"The chaps must have wanted to cheer," she said.

Ken was right: you could describe Mrs. Chapel as an old-fashioned kind of child. "I don't know about that," he said. He managed to get hold of the barman.

"Was Mr. Hurst rude to Ken?"

"I think so."

"Why didn't Ken just give him an uppercut?"

She seemed to be enjoying it all.

"Well, Hurst wasn't that rude, you know. Anyway an officer can't strike a civilian."

"And Ken would have floored him in any case."

He gave her the ginger ale and reached for his glass as fast as he decently could. "I suppose the 'various reports' you heard were pretty exaggerated, Mrs. Chapel."

"It was described as a stand-up row. You may call me Eve."

She sipped her drink like a child, the whole of her hand round the glass. Almost everything she did made him feel protective. It just wouldn't do. He said politely: "Thank you. My name is Robert."

She didn't seem to be listening. "I expect Ken is very popular with you, isn't he?"

"Yes."

He saw, suddenly, the face of Hurst in a gap between two of the boffins on the far side of the room. He didn't seem to be with anyone. What would happen if Ken were to come in here now? This was a civilian stronghold. Not that Hurst could order him out, or anything, but he might choose to make a scene just to restore the balance. If that happened, it wouldn't make things . . . Oh, *hell*. He was fed up with it, fed right up to the back teeth.

"What's his wife like?"

"I'm sorry?" She was always darting off on a fresh tack.

"Mrs. Pyne."

He studied his drink. Impatiently she asked: "Did you ever meet her?"

"Once or twice."

"What was she like?"

"Oh, a nice person."

"Ken wouldn't have married anyone not nice."

"No."

"He told me the marriage had come unstuck."

"Did he?" Ken must have told her that evening when

he'd stayed behind at the Chapel house. She'd got through that inner defense pretty fast. "I think it was just what they call incompatibility of temperament."

"Yes. How long ago was it, Robert?"

"Didn't he tell you?"

She was silent and he glanced at her and saw that he'd hurt her, and it was worse because she was trying not to show it. Without thinking he touched her hand, and she looked up, surprised.

"It was a long time ago. Some years." Her hand had felt very small.

"I see."

He drank up and looked at his watch. This was no time for finesse: he had to pull out, quick. "If you'll excuse me, I've got a stack of paper work."

"Don't be angry that I asked about him."

"The very idea! It's just that I don't know much about him. Never have." He stepped back a pace, knocking into someone, apologizing over his shoulder.

She smiled quickly. "Thank you for my ginger ale."

"We will go and have a look," said Dr. Chapel.

Whymlett thought: "We will go and see what the fairies have brought us." Chapel had made it sound just like that.

When the principal officer and the officer in scientific charge left the Instrumentation Building, Mary pressed some buttons to alter the electronic location board on the wall of her office. Anyone wanting to contact J. W. Chapel or P. K. S. Whymlett could find them in No. 1 Test Shop. From the beginning of Phase 1 onward there would arise occasions when the immediate location of key personnel became suddenly important, essential, or urgent.

The missile officer and his team were already at work in the test shop when the two scientists reached there. On their way they had talked very little. Chapel walked preoccupied. Whymlett, content in his silent company, walked beside him, taking little steps as many big men do. Before flying out from Southampton three days ago he had not seen Jim Chapel for almost two years. During this period he had worked on the development of White Lance and its electronic equipment, supervising its manufacture and directing the static-test phases on the Isle of Wight. He was now here on Tokariji as head of the specialist team responsible for the experiment. Chapel was responsible for the shoot in all its aspects: for ensuring that WL-1 was pieced together safely and correctly by his missile officer, was put into the launcher safely and correctly by his trials control and area operations officers, and was successfully fired into the atmosphere. Whymlett was responsible for the experiment: for ensuring that every one of several thousand electronic components was installed correctly in the nose cone, and that all telemetry circuits functioned perfectly during flight, to record the required data and signal it to earth for analysis.

In the years since the war Phil Whymlett had seen little of Chapel; their scientific fields had done no more than overlap. But Whymlett, from their first encounter in 1949, had found himself in contact with a man whose spirit, qualities, and scientific talent moved him beyond measure and beyond recall. Having discovered James Weyland Chapel to exist, he viewed the whole scene of scientific endeavor suddenly in a different and almost spiritual light, and could never look on it again as he had before. It had been like seeing a black-and-white drawing suddenly run with colors. For the first time in his career he had been brought to the knowledge that a scientist must live and work with nature.

He had supposed that others had understood this, long before his time and before Chapel's. Da Vinci must have understood it. But to Whymlett the revelation came as startling and he had been forced to see his work in new terms. The laboratory was no longer an air-conditioned cell in which men worked alone, cut off from their kind; it was a room with windows open to the world. The applied sciences of physics, chemistry, dynamics, and metallurgy were no longer man-devised, remote from common forms; they were tools for working with nature.

He had told his wife what had happened to him. "It was as if I'd been in a ship, knowing all about the way it was rigged and what every bit was made of—I knew the materials and what they weighed and why they had to be the shape they were; I knew all the stresses and strains and all the complicated interreactions going on between every component, and I could give you the complete breakdown in terms of physics and dynamics and the rest of it, working out graphs and computations and analyses till there wasn't anything in that ship you didn't know about, just as there was nothing *I* didn't know about. Except two things that I'd clean overlooked: that it was the wind that drove it, and the sea that kept it afloat."

This revelation had not, he thought, made any great changes for him in his career. He'd gone on plodding and come up the hard way, and wouldn't have wanted it otherwise. But his work had become more satisfying from that year onward; his few triumphs had meant more to him and his setbacks had also meant more: but he'd seen them as challenges and not frustrations and so had dealt with them more quickly. More than anything else he had been able better to judge the work of others, by watching their approach to science; he was able to spot the talented specialist who—despite his talent—would never become great, because of his limited view. And he would ally himself with the less promising, less brilliant men who were short on theory and inelegant in technique, but who knew about the wind and the sea.

His first child was born in 1950 and they gave him the

name of Jim. Chapel had never known, of course; their families had met only a few times in all those years.

Walking beside Chapel now in the mounting glare of the sunshine, he was content not to be talking. It was a miracle anyway that he was here at all, assigned to an experiment the vehicle of which had been designed by Chapel himself. He could have wished for no better thing.

They walked together toward the test shop, their steps out of unison, an ill-matched pair by appearances. Chapel, with his neat pert head and studious glasses, might have been an auctioneer's clerk; Whymlett, a much bigger man, with a broad pink face and bushy eyebrows (he'd heard it once described as "lumpy"), looked like a successful butcher. One would not have taken them for a prophet and his disciple.

"Of course you heard about BJ-9," Chapel was suddenly saying.

"I did. It was bad luck, that."

"It was bad workmanship. The point is that it left us all rather despondent. You'll notice that our people don't seem quite as lit up about WL-1 as you might expect. That will pass. White Lance is very sophisticated and the first-stage liquid fuel is remarkably nervous. We are also shooting half as high again as Blue Streak. These considerations aren't the cause of our rather glum mood; it's just the aftermath of the dumps."

"Everyone looks cheerful, to me, Jim."

"Then I expect they are. Sometimes I don't get time to look at people. I expect they're very excited." He glanced up at Whymlett and suddenly stopped walking. "It *is* exciting," he said with a tremor of passion. "It is very exciting. Half as high again. Well out beyond the ionosphere." Then he was walking quickly again. "Height isn't important, not so important—but it matters, Phil. Height matters."

More and more people came into the test shop as the principal officer and the officer in scientific charge made their first inspection of White Lance. The O.S.C. stayed with Dr. Chapel in the main bay long enough to learn that there had been no damage during transit of the hardware. Then he passed through the dust-extraction lock into the telemetry room, where the nose cone was being unpacked.

In the main bay the body of White Lance lay in its cradle, slender, seventy feet long, headless, and inert. The combustion chambers and venturi ducts had been shipped *in situ*, and the four ducts formed a red-painted cluster at the aft end of the cylinder. Men touched the outer casing with tender hands, searching for damage by feel lest the eye deceive. In their long white coats they moved in silence, with the calm of priests.

Whymlett spent an hour in the telemetry room inspecting the head component with his electronics team. Four and a half feet wide at the base, ten feet long from neck to tip, it comprised the second-stage solid-fuel motor housing, independent battery packs, command system, and massed instrumentation trays.

The head of White Lance was going to live longer than the body. The experiment was basically the same as those carried out much earlier in the Black Knight reentry physics trials. The liquid-fueled main body would push the head component nine hundred miles high into the magnetosphere; the head would then be separated by ground command, tilted through a hundred and eighty degrees to point earthward, and thrust back into the atmosphere by the second-stage solid-fuel motor. By the time the main body was falling away, exhausted of fuel and with its life-purpose completed, the head would be meeting the atmosphere and tele-recording the extreme conditions encountered: heat, shock-wave incidence, metallurgic mutations, deceleration factors, and deflection variants.

A major problem in the space-exploration program was that of reentry: the business of bringing home a manned vehicle through the atmosphere without its burning up. The era of the parachute descent was over: manned space shots were becoming ambitious, and the idea of landing large-crew capsules by parachute—even by cluster parachutes—was no longer worth a look. The problem held out two main solutions, each the opposite of the other in terms of approach: you could study and practice methods of bringing the capsule home slowly, reducing the friction factor; and you could study the chances of designing a capsule that would resist white heat and protect the crew inside it.

The head of WL-1 was a stand-in for such a crew. In the plunge to earth at a speed of four thousand m.p.h. it would record its experience and speak of what it knew in the final seconds of its life. It had taken Whymlett and his team two years to build this brain; once launched, it would live for seventeen minutes; of those seventeen minutes it could be given only three and a half in which to fulfill its purpose as it rammed into the thickening atmospheric belt and signaled its findings there. Then it would crash, a burnt-out skull, on 'Covery.

It would be months before these findings could be analyzed and understood. Massed data would be accumulated on magnetic tape, film, and penned record; the digital and analogue computers would provide upward of two thousand salient facts from an original source of half a million data points correct to five decimal places.

By that time WL-1 would be a heap of decaying fragments, the subject of an autopsy by the metallurgists. Then it would be junked. Stressed metal is not used again. The epitaph would take the usual form: "White Lance? She's gone to 'Covery."

The men working among the complex array of instrumentation trays did not think about that. White Lance had only just come into existence, to be nurtured and set alive. They worked as delicately as surgeons tending the exposed nerves of a brain.

Earlier this morning the solid-fuel cuckoo motor for the head component had been taken from the fire-safe blockhouse and set up in No. 5 Test Shop more than a mile distant from No. 1. There was no building anywhere near. No. 5 Test Shop was used only for the handling of dangerous components, and the place had already been cleared of non-essential personnel. Those who remained were the acceptance, project, and ground safety officers, with the contract specialist and his team. They were working on the motor now.

It was the least complicated component in the whole of the White Lance makeup, a thick tubular mass of heavily packed explosive inside a polished casing, with a housing for the igniter. It was already held rigid on a test-mounting by restraining gear to guard against vibration. (The danger sequence was simple enough: vibration—friction—spark.) While the men removed the blanking plug from the venturi the ground safety officer watched, standing alone on the fringe of the activity, sometimes moving to get a better view, sometimes glancing at the face of a technician. Mostly he watched their hands for signs of nervousness, fatigue, or sweat. From the left wrist of every man there trailed an armored cable to a grounding rail that ran the length of the shop; a wire ran from every tool they used. The static electricity on Tokariji could produce a half-inch spark.

A notice was spelled out along the wall in red letters three feet high. CALM—CLEANLINESS—CARE. The G.S.O. stood watching, a calm, clean-looking, and careful man whose every movement was deliberate and slow. He watched the cuckoo motor and the technicians with quiet contemplation, as he had many times watched the disarming of mines and unexploded bombs on the south coast of England years ago. Under the authority of the P.O., Tokariji, his word was law. He could stop any operation at the drop of his hand; he could order a week's work to be done again; he could, if he saw fatigue in a man, send him to bed, even if that man were the key technician of a process impossible to continue without him. A lay visitor to No. 5 Test Shop had once asked him what would happen, on a small island like this, if a solid-fuel motor was ignited by accident. The careful eyes had brooded, and the careful voice had said: "Not many would live."

Walking back to his office with Phil Whymlett, Chapel looked around at the buildings and range-head instrumentation posts. Now and then a voice called across from a kinetheodolite unit to the next, where the vehicle-tracking network was undergoing checks. The establishment messenger went unhurriedly past on his bicycle. Somewhere a Diesel engine throbbed quietly.

"It feels good," said Chapel. "This is the first-day's feeling. You wouldn't notice it, because you're a stranger here. People are quiet, but it's a different quietness now. They are becoming absorbed."

They stood for a moment in the shade of a building, and Whymlett said nothing but looked about him as Chapel was doing. The sun made a glare along white walls; the wind sock at the end of the airstrip hung slack; the ocean was grape-blue and still.

"It's the feeling that always comes, on the early days of the first phase. But it's always new, as the morning is always new. There is another thing. Even so soon, there is the feeling that there was never a time when White Lance wasn't here with us in our midst."

They walked on toward the Instrumentation Building,

and still Whymlett did not answer. He was content to know what Jim was talking about: the wind and the sea.

Before they reached the building Chapel stopped again abruptly and stared into his face; and Whymlett was shocked to hear the note of stridency that had come to this man's voice.

"Nothing must stop us. Nothing must go wrong. Nothing."

Chapter 11

Whymlett had been an hour at the house and it was almost midnight.

"I should be going, Evie."

"Stay till he comes."

"All right."

In the last week the moon had grown big, and they sat on the veranda in its light. Sometimes he got out of the cane chair and leaned on the rail, and she watched his bulky silhouette against the moon track on the ocean. Minutes passed in silence again, and they made no effort to talk. They had hit it off on the day of his arrival, and every evening he had come to the house and she had listened to their talk of the day's work. Tonight Jim was later than usual, and Phil told her there was a Phase 2 coordination conference still going on in the P.O.'s office. She had asked him to go over there and try breaking it up, but he was shocked at the idea.

He had changed, she thought, already, in the few days she had known him. His earlier mood of quiet satisfaction had left him, and now he had to make an effort to pretend it wasn't so.

As he came and sat down again she said in the pale light: "It's not going well, is it, Phil?"

"Going fine."

"Is it just a routine crop of trouble, or something un-expected?"

His cane chair creaked as he shifted in it uneasily. "You can't get a rocket up—a big one—without meeting snags along the way."

"Jim won't talk to me about it, and now even you won't."

He thought it was bad that she had to say that, to use the word "even." But it was true; Jim never said much to her in company; he probably said even less when they were alone.

"It's no good any of us telling you we've found a point 03-degree error in the turbine-reactor valve trunnions. Would it mean anything to you? Don't think I'm being patronizing."

"What is the margin?"

He swung his head to look at her. "Margin?"

"Don't be dishonest with me, Phil." She was suddenly leaning forward, closer to him. "You forget that I spend a lot of my life listening to technical discussions, playing the perfect scientist's wife—always at hand and as well-groomed as I can manage, never interrupting with silly questions." The bitterness had come into her voice before she knew it. "So I pick up quite a lot of rocket lore, in my job—I've only to hear a phrase spoken fifty times and I remember it. And the phrase I'm talking about now is 'the margin of error.' Stop me if I'm wrong, but with the design of almost every component there's a degree or two of toleration. A thousandth of an inch out and it's all right; another thousandth, and the thing has to be rebuilt or scrapped or whatever it is. I'm right, aren't I?"

He had looked away from her. The awful thing was that she had grasped the whole situation that had come up early this morning. It was intuition. It was knowing about the wind and the sea without knowing about the ship itself. He was awed and uneasy.

"So I'll ask you again," she said. "With this turbine thing, what is the margin of error?"

"Point 05." It was no good dodging. She'd got it.

"And the actual error is point 03. So you're well within the margin. And Jim won't tolerate it." She leaned back.

It was a minute before Whymlett spoke. "Did he talk to you about it, Evie?"

"No. Not about that particularly. But I know what's on his mind—he's afraid of failure."

He remembered the sudden stridency in Jim's tone: *Nothing must go wrong.*

"Jim's right. He works to one rule. Perfection."

"He can't, and you know it. Nobody can. You can work to one ten-thousandth of an inch, and be satisfied; but it's not perfect. Perfection is beyond a millionth, beyond uncountable millionths. That's why you stipulate a margin of error, isn't it? This turbine thing, Phil—how long will it take to get it right? I mean to get it accurate enough for Jim?"

He said overcasually, "Oh, a day or two."

"You're cheating again. You don't know how long it's going to take, because you don't know how much accuracy he's going to insist on. Do you?"

She too had changed and her own words surprised her; she had never talked so directly about Jim to anyone, even to the wives of other scientists on Tokariji. Her loyalty to Jim was weakening and it worried her; but there was a headiness in using for the first time the power to criticize, and it wasn't easy to stop.

"Why is he so apprehensive, Phil? What does he think is going to go wrong with White Lance?"

He stood up again restlessly, thrusting his hands into his pockets, looking down at her in the milky light. "It's just first-shoot nerves. That's what they call it here—you must have heard the phrase, because I have, in the last few days.

Jim designed this one and it's never been flight-tested. Surely to God that's enough?"

There were footsteps and she didn't answer.

Chapel was walking quickly along the tamarisk hedge, and Whymlett knew that he had won the day.

"We do it again, Phil. I convinced them." The moon was reflected across his glasses as he stood on the step of the veranda looking up. "I hoped you'd still be here so that I could tell you."

"It's good to hear, Jim." He tried to sound really glad. He wished Evie hadn't said any of those things, especially that Jim was afraid of failure. What did she know about the difficulties of preparing for a big shoot? It hadn't been—he thought now—intuition on her part; she didn't know about the wind and the sea or even the ship; but she knew the captain and knew that Jim was a perfectionist. Why wasn't she glad, and proud? There weren't many in this world like Jim.

"It took a little persuasion," Chapel said. His hands fumbled about in his jacket pockets; he was embarrassed, perhaps, to sound so triumphant. "But it's all clear now." Whymlett knew they'd been at it for three hours in the Instrumentation Building.

Evie had said nothing; nor had Jim spoken to her; he hadn't looked at her.

"We're both very glad," Whymlett said, and turned his head to her. "Aren't we?"

She got up and the small bracelet of shells on her wrist shimmered in the moonlight. "Will it mean a long delay, Jim?"

He looked up at her for the first time. "I don't think of it in terms of delay."

"But they do. The others."

"We have to get things right. There's no other consideration."

"I don't think," Whymlett said, "Evie quite understands. After all—"

"Yes, I understand." She faced him with a swing of her bare shoulders. "But the things I understand might not be the things that you do. I'm not talking about turbines or anything. I mean things like obsession." Then with her odd habit of changing the subject she said: "Jim will be wanting a hot milk nightcap, Phil. Some for you, too?"

"It's late, and I must go along."

In the doorway she half-turned and said to him: "I don't want Jim to be hurt by White Lance. Or by anything."

The episode of the keys came at a bad time because Phase 2 had begun and the preparation sequence was claiming everyone's attention. Only to one man—Hurst—did the episode seem relevant; he was therefore one of the few who managed to keep their tempers.

The keys belonged to an office in the film library and they were reported missing on the morning of Day 1, Phase 2; this was the day following Chapel's successful conference on the error in the turbine system.

Hurst, as chief security officer, was vested with all powers to conduct a full-scale search for the missing keys, but as it was always a matter looked upon as urgent he reported to the principal officer immediately.

This was his third visit to Dr. Chapel since the day, a week ago, when Colonel Pyne had sent him out of the army area under escort. That same day he had gone to the principal officer and complained of this treatment.

Chapel had listened carefully and when Hurst had finished he had asked: "Had you permission to enter army territory, Mr. Hurst?"

"I assumed I had the right, sir, as security officer for the whole of Tokariji."

"There I can't advise you. But whether or not you had

the right, it seems reasonable to suppose that Colonel Pyne, as the officer in charge of a weapon still on the secret list, would have his own security arrangements. I suggest you take it up with your Ministry."

Hurst had not persisted. He had expected support from the P.O. against the head of what amounted to a foreign element on the island; and he had not got it. But there would be no point in pursuing the matter. Dr. Chapel was never known to change his mind. Hurst had turned quietly to an interesting question: why had Chapel sided with Pyne, a man he was known to dislike?

Hurst's second visit was again on the subject of Pyne.

"Quite unofficially, sir, I'd like to make a suggestion. You're the highest authority here and you should be informed of everything that goes on. I'm right about that much, I know."

He had waited for some encouragement. Chapel had said nothing. Hurst was obliged to be direct.

"My suggestion is that you should personally inspect the solid-fuel motor that was delivered to Pyne's unit three days ago."

After a long silence Chapel had asked: "Why?"

"I think it might interest you."

"Please be explicit, Mr. Hurst."

"That's all I'm saying."

"If you feel disposed to give me a good reason for your suggestion, I shall consider acting upon it."

Again it was the final word. Hurst had not persisted. It was never his policy. It would go on confidential record that 1) he had lodged a complaint concerning Colonel Pyne's high-handed treatment of him, and 2) he had suggested to the P.O. that he should inspect the solid-fuel motor delivered to the army unit. It would go on record also that in neither case did the P.O. take any action.

His third visit to Dr. Chapel was required in principle. He

expected nothing to transpire directly from such a formality, and nothing did. The P.O. simply thanked him for his report and asked him to make full and immediate enquiries.

Hurst began at the film library. The keys belonged to a small filing office handling very little secret documentation. This made no difference. The rule was clear on the subject. Immediate search must be made for any keys missing from any technical section of whatever category; a security guard must be mounted at the door to which such keys belonged; and a new lock must be fitted the moment when it was decided that the keys were beyond immediate recovery.

The outcome was that Hurst spent the entire day instituting the search and making his enquiries. He knew that it was impossible that such enquiries would not turn up irrelevant items of information that might prove useful to him, whether the keys were found or not. It was a good chance for him to plow up the ground and he used it to the full, so that by the end of the morning he was being cursed in every section.

The person most aware of the unrest was Mary White, because in time of crisis the principal officer was always in demand and it was part of her job to calm people down and explain that he couldn't be disturbed except by real emergencies. Her telephones and the big personnel-location board together made a sensitive sounding instrument, and she could almost draw a graph showing the temper of the whole establishment at any given time.

Today the line had dipped. The P.O. believed that last night's conference had gone well; everyone else except Mr. Whymlett said it had gone badly. The chief of the Mods and Rectification team had put it: "We're going to rub out a point 03 tolerated error at the cost of a point 9 delay in the sequence—everybody smile, please." This setback wasn't important by itself; it was a measure of the P.O.'s attitude to White Lance. He was going to narrow the margin of error all the way through, and that could mean a setback totaling weeks.

Now the security officer was going through every section, interrupting the work. The No. 1 telephone in Mary's office buzzed again every time she put it down.

"The P.O. there?"

"He's deep in it, Mr. Johnson."

"Just knock on the door for me, just this once, there's a good girl. Ask him to get Hurst out of my hair. Who runs this show anyway?"

"I'll take it up with him the moment I can."

It worried her. Day 1, Phase 2, was too early for crises, too early by far.

Within two minutes of talking to Mrs. Chapel, Hurst sensed a change in her. She had never liked him but had never let it show. This morning it showed.

He had known precisely where to find her. As on many occasions he had driven back from the north shore of the island well ahead of her; this morning he had gone as far as the security office, turned the car, and was driving toward the living quarters as she came down the road on her bicycle. The field glasses were on the seat beside him but it didn't matter if she noticed them; they were usually there, a tool of his trade.

He stopped the car and was standing beside it when she came up. "Can you give me a moment, Mrs. Chapel?"

She skidded on the powdering of sand and stood astride the crossbar. Below the short sleeves of her overalls the salt had dried white on her arms. She could not see his eyes behind the sunglasses.

"I expect you've heard about the missing keys?"

"Yes I have, Mr. Hurst."

"They've got to be found, of course. You meet a lot of people in the day." A flat bright smile. "Any clues?"

"Are they so important?"

"If they weren't, we wouldn't bother to use them, would we? These belong to one of the rooms in the film library, and there are still plenty of records in there of the BJ-9 shoot. Now this particular room's in charge of Miss Jebb, and you have quite a lot to do with the female personnel, don't you?"

It was a term she disliked; there was nothing wrong with calling them women.

"Don't you trust Miss Jebb?"

"I don't trust anyone." The quick clever smile didn't take the edge off; it made it worse.

"Not even me?" Instantly she wished not to have said that. It had been meant as a challenge but it had sounded arch; the tone was arrogant enough but the words were wrong; it should have been: "Myself included?"

"Not even you, Mrs. Chapel." He was standing close to her, and spoke very softly as if they were sharing an intimate secret. "People act on their motives, you see, and they're motivated by subconscious drives, and no one can do anything about it." She leaned the bicycle away as far as she could. "Haven't you ever done anything that made you wonder why you did it? Oh, you'll have a ready answer—you'll rationalize quick as a flash—but it won't necessarily be the true reason. Only your subconscious knows that, and your subconscious won't always tell." He smiled impishly.

He was so close that she could smell the sweat on his body. That alone was enough to give her a subconscious drive to get away from him.

"Mr. Hurst, I hate keys and the whole idea of keys, because I like trusting people. I can't tell you how many keys I've lost myself—that's elementary psychology, too, isn't it? It's probably the same with Miss Jebb. You may have a hard job finding these, because you're going the wrong way about it."

She rode off and he didn't try to stop her.

It hadn't been correct. The principal officer's wife should support the chief security officer in his difficult task and give him every cooperation, both moral and practical—and so on and so forth. It wouldn't have to matter. She was different now. Everything was different now, and rather frightening.

Chapter 12

Four weeks after their arrival on Tokariji the army unit
put up a trials shoot of all six Javelin 33s. Colonel Pyne had
briefed them some days earlier but the wind had been
wrong, blowing softly from the east. As soon as it veered
through south to southwest he ordered the trials mounted.
The thick white smoke would now be blown toward the
northeast area of the island where there were no buildings.

The Javelins were short-range ground-to-ground tactical
missiles, slender and potent with triple fins and venturi de-
flectors that sent the smoke fanning out in a ring as they left
the ramp. The echoes came blasting back from the civilian
establishment buildings, and the men appreciated the sound
and its fierceness. This was what they were for.

As an administrator Major Nash had nothing much to do
with the trials, but stood watching from the south rim of the
weapon pit, lifting his field glasses to track each missile as far
as he could before it was lost in the glare of blue. Noting
how the men worked at the ramp and how the C.O. kept
clear of them so as not to fuss them, Nash decided this was
the best day the unit had spent on Tokariji. In the last three
weeks the morale had slowly healed.

Ken had not refound his normal self. His reserve was
stronger than ever, almost impenetrable, but unless you tried
to reach him with an unwise question or forgot for a moment

that he was the C.O. he was easy to live with again. There was even a new aspect to him that worried Nash sometimes —it was a show of defiance, an almost gay defiance, and it came out in a word or a gesture when you were least ready for it. Yesterday Nash had heard Stoner report an increased deposit of early-morning sea mist on the Triton's ditalium-alloy casing, and Ken had said: "Sea mist? Wipe it off with a mop. It'll take more than a bit of sea mist to worry that beauty."

Completely out of character. Ken would normally have issued new standing orders: entire casing and external ancillary pods to be inspected for encrustation daily, antihumidity shrouds to be rigged at weapon officer's discretion, special watchfulness to be maintained at times of wind change and barometer fluctuation.

This precautionary drill was in fact practiced, but it hadn't been on the C.O.'s personal orders; Stoner had arranged it himself.

Another thing: Ken was now getting through a good half-bottle every night, either in the mess bar or his room. It didn't show, except to those few who knew him well. It didn't, you could say, affect him at all—he was always in perfect command of himself. There was, though, just a fraction more of the gay defiance in him when the bottle was down to half.

Nash had told no one that he was worried by Ken's new mood. After a couple of weeks he got used to it and worried less. Today, with the white smoke pouring across the terrain and the smooth fierce rush of the missiles probing skyward in the sun, he felt that all was to rights again and life worth living. The change in Ken had been noticed throughout the unit—the boys missed nothing; they had you in a spotlight the whole time. But the new C.O. seemed as good as the old one, and they were ready to work with him.

The day itself also went right, and all missile cases were retrieved from the yellow-stain areas that were spread in a

line at thirty miles' range across the ocean northward. By
15.00 hours the pickup launch was back in harbor; by 18.00
the missiles had been dried, cleaned, examined, rearmed, triggered, and disarmed again and arrayed on the "first-alert"
racks in the weapon pit, and Ken had ordered a pint all round
and challenged Wilson to a hundred break on the baize.

The personal gods of Robert Nash were no less generous
that night. Walking from the senior mess to the little Telex
building in the civilian establishment, where there was a
twice-daily world news handout, he met Eve Chapel on her
way over to the guesthouse and talked to her for nearly half
an hour, saying nothing important, just strolling in the soft
light of the stars and calling her "Eve," as she had allowed
him.

She had seen the Javelins go up, with what she described
as "daunting precision," and he was delighted. Maybe the
whole civilian establishment would now see that there was
a fully operational missile unit on Tokariji instead of a bunch
of men with a few dummy rounds to look after.

"How's White Lance?" he asked her. "You must be getting
near blast-off by now."

He knew they were meeting a rough sequence of snags—
the talk among the boffins in the mess was dispiriting to listen
to these days; but he wanted to cheer her up if he could.

"The whole establishment's getting near to blast-off," she
said with a soft laugh. "I expect they'll weather it in the end
but at the moment we're set at stormy."

"The more snags in preparation, the smoother the shoot.
It's like that every time we have to put up a new type." He
could say it cockily, as second-in-command of a unit noted
for its daunting precision.

"I'm not worried, Robert."

"Oh. That's fine."

"There's nothing I can do to help, you see. They're un-
approachable at this stage, and apart from a glass of hot milk

or a clean pair of socks there's nothing they need from me."
They stood now on the unit boundary in the glow from the
radio-mast lamps. The night was calm. "Or there's nothing
I can give them," she said quietly. "That's different, but it
works out just the same. I watch those lights every night—
the wall of the room glows red with them."

He looked up at the mast, something in him delighted at
the way she had changed the subject on a breath, and at the
fact that he remembered it was her habit.

He said: "We see it, too. We're just underneath them."

"I know."

He looked down at her. The color of the lights darkened
her brown skin and her eyes were clear and shining.

"You give them more than you think, Eve. They know
you're here and they can see you around. They're lucky."

"You are too gallant, Major." But he could tell she wasn't
laughing at his ineloquence.

They walked together as far as the guesthouse and he was
careful to keep a little distance from her side because quite a
few people passed them and acknowledged her. She let him
hold her hand for longer than was necessary when they said
good night, and he was as careful to say: "Please give Dr.
Chapel the respectful good wishes of all of us. We're sure
that White Lance will go splendidly on the day."

Walking back to the unit in the drowsy air, lulled by his
thoughts of her, he remembered vaguely that she had not
once mentioned Ken.

The message came through a couple of hours after sunup
and the signals clerk took it straight across to the C.O.'s
office.

"He's not here," said Sergeant Lacey. He looked at the
uncoded signal slip, read it twice and went next door to see
the adjutant.

Major Nash was hearing a request for compassionate leave.

Company Sergeant-major Rice told Sergeant Lacey to wait outside.

"Looks urgent, sir."

The C.S.M. read the slip and put it on the adjutant's desk. Major Nash broke off the hearing and asked Rice: "Where's the C.O.?"

"I last saw him in his vehicle, sir. Took the east road half an hour ago."

"Tell Sar'nt Lacey to get transport and find the C.O. immediately and give him the signal. Tell Foster to acknowledge signal received."

Lacey was trotting across to the M.T. bay when he heard the sound of an engine and looked up to see a trail of ocher-colored dust along the east road. He trotted back to intercept the C.O. on the slip track past the huts.

Colonel Pyne got out of the Land-Rover and touched a rock to get rid of static. His swimming trunks were hanging from one of the width indicators to dry. He took the slip from Lacey, checked the time of his receipt with his watch, worked things out, and handed back the slip. "Get it acknowledged. Where's Mr. Stoner?"

"In the pit, sir. Arming drill."

Pyne walked over the fifty yards of rock shale and went down the ladder from the south rim. The shadow of the Triton lay in a dark bar across the pit.

"Mr. Stoner! Immediate camouflage drill, please."

Captain Stoner responded with as much grace as he could muster. Half the solid-fuel Javelin motors were out of the pods and the igniter gear was uncovered. The C.O. was already going back up the ladder.

"Right. Thompson—three men remain. Stow motors and gear, the rest on the nets and makee sharp work now!"

The boys were happy enough. Arming drill was a bloody great bore and they could do it in their sleep.

"One minute twenty seconds!" Stoner was calling. "Beat that record, now!"

It took a minute thirty because they were out of practice. Camouflage drill was conveniently overlooked in the main training program, because in this place even a light wind lifted powdered sand in the air and the net was often covered with it. A third of the causes of missile malfunction was traceable to the presence of grit in vital components. But the order had been given and two men were already at the winch handles. The Rossiter Type A weapon-pit camouflage gear was simple and effective: a steel rail ran full circle below the rim, and the net was in two halves. Hand winches drew the net by cable, much as a curtain is drawn, until the two halves met and the pit was totally covered like a circus tent. The "mushroom" was then put up in the center, hoisted by winch and lanyard until the length of the missile was sheathed in a sleeve of canvas and topped by a camouflage dish on the umbrella principle. From the rim of the dish there hung streamers, kept motionless in low-wind conditions by lead sinkers.

In one minute thirty seconds the Triton and weapon pit had vanished, and from a point as near as the Instrumentation Building in the civilian establishment it looked as if a large storehouse stood in their place.

Corporal Thompson and his three arming-crew were now smothered in fine sand; but the motors were already safe in stowage and the igniter gear was protected.

Captain Stoner had stood frowning at his watch during the operation, but there was no point in telling the boys they'd lost ten seconds with it. The winches had worked and that alone was a marvel; some enterprising hero must have been keeping them clear of sand. He made for the ladder in the weird gloom under the net and climbed through the manhole into the heat of the sun. The bloody thing was up and he hoped Ken was satisfied and would kindly tell him when they could take the bloody thing down again.

Colonel Pyne was in his office, sitting alone at the desk. His amber eyes regarded Stoner with more than usual reserve.

"Take what down?"

"The net," Stoner said.

"Is it rigged?"

"You gave the order a few minutes ago." Ken didn't seem to be with it at all.

"I know I gave the order. Are you reporting that it is now carried out?"

"Yes, sir."

"Then all you do now is wait for the order to take the net down again." He gazed at and through Stoner.

"Right." He turned for the door.

Ken's voice was suddenly more alert. He'd emerged from his woolgathering. "We may have to leave it up for some hours. It's a good opportunity to get the sand off it. Give it a beating. Jump on it or something. But it will remain in place until you have my personal orders to take it down." He gazed up at the lieutenant from beneath his brows. "That is important."

"Understood."

Stoner went out.

Give it a beating. Jump on it or something. Particularly or something. If anyone asked him if he'd seen the C.O. this morning, he would say: Yes. If anyone asked him what kind of mood the C.O. was in, he would say: Since you ask, I will be frank. I am buggered if I know.

A door opened along the passage and the voice of C.S.M. Rice went ricocheting from wall to wall:

"*H'about*' . . . *tun! Quee*-eek . . . *much!*"

Private Samuels was propelled verbally into the passage, doing his best to pretend that he was made of clockwork. Compassionate leave granted. There'd been no question, of course. It was quads. Four of them. Strike a light, nobody'd ever be able to say he'd got no lead in his pencil!

Colonel Pyne waited until the tramp of boots had passed his door and left the building in peace, then leaned well back in his chair, his half-closed eyes moving from one knot to another in the pinewood wall.

The signal had read:

Unidentified reconnaissance aircraft overhead Wake Island 09.21 hours altitude 82,000 feet estimated speed 320 knots heading your direction please acknowledge and report details if sighted.

Should the aircraft be observing Wake Island by telephoto its speed would be reduced to at least half. Should it subsequently head across Tokariji it would increase speed to something like six hundred knots between the two objectives before slowing again. The distance was nine hundred and thirty sea miles. Should Tokariji in fact be a second objective it would arrive overhead in roughly ninety minutes.

The figures of the calculation suddenly seemed to dissolve in his mind, and all he could see were the small colored shells. For a moment he let the image linger, then the figures and their significance came back and he sat straighter in the chair to deal with them. There was the telephone, on the desk, and he must use it. The unit had no instrument for tracking anything that high, but the civilian establishment could track Mars and Venus as a matter of routine. You could manage without a high-clearance loader but this was on a different scale.

It was impossible of course to speak directly to the principal officer. There must be scruples—for the love of God there must be a sense of decency to leaven the black shame. One was not a total barbarian.

He lifted the receiver.

Chapter 13

"Your glasses, Dr. Chapel."

He stopped and looked down at her. "Oh yes."

She gave them to him and watched him go out. The smoked lenses were made to clip on over his seeing glasses, and he always forgot them, so she kept them on her desk and reminded him every time. There were three spare pairs in her drawer; he lost them at the rate of one a week.

He was not wearing his jacket so she went into his office and took it down, brushing the chalk from the elbows and cuffs, worrying quietly about him. Day 4, Phase 3, was beginning as badly as most days now began, and already his face had a drawn look. With the preparation sequence almost two weeks behind schedule, White Lance was on this day going into the launcher, if nothing went wrong.

She believed that nothing would go wrong if they all heeded him, and obeyed him, and kept their faith in him through this long day; she believed also that they would not do this. Only one of them felt as she did. Mr. Whymlett had told her last night:

"They'll have to be big-minded tomorrow, Mary. Until they grow their minds big enough to see that he knows what he's doing—and to let him do it—they'll hit one snag after another. But they won't damn well see it yet."

The O.S.C. was a changed man, unrecognizable after

four weeks here, terse, brooding, critical. But he had kept his faith in Dr. Chapel. Oddly, Dr. Chapel did not know this; he was blind to criticism and approval alike; he had lost sight of people and could see only White Lance.

Four or five of the telemetry crew had already been sent to the establishment psychologist by the ground safety officer. Two of them had made a scene in the mess the night before last, shouting at each other; a trivial argument about link-system principles had led to a public row that had done nobody any good.

Young Follett, the missile officer, had said to someone in Mary's hearing: "Of course there's a consolation. White Lance is fourteen days behind schedule, but she's a hundred per cent correct in every single component. If she stays that way she'll go like a dream when we shoot—it'll go into the records as a classic success. But in the process the P.O.'s going to send half the establishment home as certifiable nut cases. I really mean that. So it's a hell of a consolation, isn't it?"

There were one or two people still solid behind the project and thus indirectly behind the P.O. Mr. Whymlett, of course, and Alec Griggs, and the ground safety officer. There was room for more like those.

The No. 1 telephone rang again and she hung up the jacket and answered it. The switchboard told her the call was from the army unit. The voice that followed was a quiet growl. While she listened to it she pushed two buttons to change the personnel-location board: J. W. Chapel to Launcher.

"Yes, Colonel Pyne. Do you want me to make it a personal report to the principal officer?"

"He should be informed, I think. The main thing is that your Instrumentation people should have my request, as soon as possible, to track any aircraft overhead the island at about 10.45 hours and to let me have the details—height, speed, and direction. I'm sorry to trouble you with this but we have no equipment."

It was the voice of a man, she thought, who didn't find it easy to apologize. "I'm sure the principal officer would want to help you in any way possible, Colonel. I'll contact Instrumentation at once."

"Thank you. There is something further. Any reconnaissance of Tokariji will naturally be of interest to Security, so that your security officer should be told. The signal I received was not coded, so I see no objection to passing it on to the proper quarters. Have you a pencil handy?"

She wrote down the message as he gave it to her. When he had rung off she contacted the Contraves, F.P.S. 16, Baker-Nunn, and Link-System units one after another. They had nothing to do until the WL-1 shoot rehearsal began in a week's time and they would be glad of a little action. If any aircraft passed overhead the island at 10.45 hours, at whatever height, it would be caught like a moth in a searchlight.

She could still hear in her mind, a long time afterward, the voice of Colonel Pyne. It had a peculiar resonance. There had also sounded a note of reluctance to every word he had said, as if he were for some reason obliged to treaty with an enemy.

These men had a different look. It was more than fatigue, though they were fatigued; it was more than worry, though they were worried.

From the beginning of this phase the routine observation of every man in the establishment was stepped up by two people particularly: Dr. Friedmann, the psychologist, and Irving, the ground safety officer. As he went into No. 1 Test Shop soon after sunrise, Irving greeted the first arrivals and summed up his private view of things.

These men looked different today from what they had

looked a month ago because they were getting tired, and because the tensions beginning a month ago had now built up in them and they knew there would be no release for yet another month. They looked like this because they had struck problems by the hundred and had overcome them; it was the overcoming of them that had left its mark. And they knew there would be more ahead. They looked different not only from how they had looked but also from the way they should look. White Lance was in good shape; you could double every error in five or six hundred installations without hitting the margin; there had probably never been a missile so close, at this stage, to perfection. So they should be looking confident—tired but confident of their ability to weather another month of strain; they should be looking satisfied—tired but satisfied that whatever problems came up in the future, those that had come up in the past had been beaten. But they didn't look confident or satisfied. You would expect them to but they didn't: and that was the difference you were really seeing—between what should be and what was.

The day was starting badly. Already Irving had had to remind three technicians to ground themselves as they came into the test shop, and one of them had told him to go to hell, so he had sent him straight to Dr. Friedmann with a threat of indefinite suspension if he failed to report there.

Outside the test shop a light wind rose, and that too was bad; wind brought two enemies of any missile: sand and salt. The Meteorology Building had reported that the wind would drop by noon. The feeling was that it would have to, whatever the Met. said, because today White Lance was going into the launch area.

The specialist team from Wymark-Vincent, the builders of WL-1, had finished installing their electronics trays, and all functional tests on the first-stage motor shutdown and tank-rupture circuits had been carried out. Irving had signed his ground safety officer's certificate: White Lance was physically in safe condition to undergo the controlled explosion of a static-firing test on the launcher.

Before noon the wind had not dropped but it was decided to continue operations. The missile was hoisted into the eighty-foot transporter and bolted down in its cradle; and as it was taken at a crawl over the two miles of macadam track to the launch area, Project White Lance passed into Phase 4.

Irving watched the little drifts of sand and sniffed at the salty air. By tonight the missile would be erect and exposed. The wind sang among the instrumentation antennae and even in the sunlight its sound was eerie. He knew the men disliked it. They were scientists and technicians, materialists, most of them atheists; but superstition is in all men, because man differs from animal in that he has imagination. Here on this island remote in the ocean, in an atmosphere of mounting stress, even these men became subtly attuned to imagery and prey to groundless fears; and fear was a prime cause of accident proneness.

Irving's sphere was technical; he was trained in chemistry, metallurgy, electricity, and physics, and knew what metals must not touch others, what conditions could set up a spark; but he was trained also in psychology and understood the mechanics of man at work. The behavior of every technician must be noted in the record book, now more carefully than before. Already he had recommended changes in the personnel because of accident proneness, fatigue, and "discipline resistance"—a term for bloody-mindedness—and several men had been reassigned to tasks as important but less exacting; an electronics foreman had been sent home to England for a month's vacation on full pay; in the High-test Peroxide fuel-handling team a chemist had been suspended after a second slight mistake and had agreed with the decision, knowing himself that for some reason he was becoming accident prone. There would be an increase in such cases as the weeks ran out.

The G.S.O. recognized the familiar pattern. Project White Lance had gathered hundreds of men—each with his own distinct personality—into a special kind of crowd, a corporate body that had its own existence and that was an entity in itself. Irving had often talked to the establishment psychologist about this, and Friedmann had said:

"It's true of any major shoot. There are two components: the men and their missile. The men come to surrender their individual identities to the corporate body. As the tensions of one phase lead to the greater tensions of the next, a crisis—very comparable to a fever—is set up, and the corporate body becomes sick."

Friedmann had leaned on the edge of his desk, a thin pale man with large eyes and a hesitant smile.

"It becomes healthily sick, and this is necessary. Without this fever you wouldn't get a squib off the ground, any more than you'd move an audience of a thousand people to laughter or tears if the actors didn't bring their suppressed first-night frenzy onto the stage. Then we have the other component, the missile, and we have the relationship between them. They are not unlike a blind man and his dog. The missile is the blind man and the human group is the dog. A trained guide dog recognizes his master as an extension of his own body joined by the harness. If the man strikes a lamppost or a curbstone the dog's own body feels the shock. It's the only explanation of a guide dog's astonishing ability to keep its master from harm. The man is a part of the dog, and in the same way a missile becomes a part of the corporate body—an extension of the group. You know better than I do that a mishap in the work on any component during the preparation sequence is felt throughout the establishment."

Irving had seen it happen many times. The sequence began

with the feeling that the hardware team could look after the main-body installations, and the electronics team could see to the telemetry circuits, and any mistakes made would be contained in a watertight compartment. Within days this feeling changed, as the teams became merged psychologically, and each became more aware of the others. The corporate body had begun to breathe of its own.

"With White Lance," Friedmann had said quietly, "we have another factor, chief of which is the attitude of Dr. Chapel. His attitude to the missile—which he designed himself—is one of obsessional devotion, a delicate balance between the fear of failure and the will to succeed. It's a struggle within his psyche, of great proportions. He has to win it and the terrible thing is that he has to win it against himself."

You could think too much about this, Irving warned himself as he followed the transporter to the launch area. Chapel was Principal Officer, Tokariji, at the head of many specialist teams. The picture wasn't pretty: a head, at odds with itself, on a corporate body in which fever raged . . . It mustn't be thought about in those terms, though they were true. You had to understand them, accept them, and forget them consciously, letting the subconscious direct your every action on the basis of those terms, and make sure that whether White Lance left the launcher or not, nobody would be hurt.

Make sure they lived by the rules; it was all you could hope to do. Calm—Cleanliness—Care. Keep your hair on, watch out for dirt, and take it steady.

The sand rose and drifted, powdering out behind the huge tires of the transporter. A dozen men walked with it, keeping pace. Irving went suddenly ahead to kick a stone aside; a tire, meeting a stone with its edge, could flick it away with a bullet's force.

Most of the army unit were lining the ridge thrown up

by the excavation of the weapon pit. The transporter was passing some half-mile away and they stared across at the naked shine of the missile. They were a little in awe of their own ICBM, the Triton; they had never handled a weapon of such size. Now they looked upon White Lance, four times as long, and said nothing of what they felt, being too engrossed. Experienced in rocketry, they could no longer see a missile as a motionless object. They saw what this one would look like as it left the earth, and could find nothing adequate to say about it.

The G.S.O., walking among the technicians along the macadam track, listened with half his mind to their talk. It was desultory and formless:

If this bloody wind kept up they'd never get her into the launcher by tonight. The Met. was usually wrong. What was that about a recco plane over Toka this morning? Trust Hurst to organize a security panic at a time like this! What state was the P.O. in today? Same state we're all in, sweating HTP.

Sand came up from their shoes.

When the transporter reached the gantry its engine was cut off, and Irving looked about him. A few minutes ago the final alert had sounded over the whole network and from now on all authorized traffic in Area 1 was ordered to reduce speed to 10 m.p.h. No other traffic was to pass within the safety perimeter boundary fifty yards from the gantry. Every man in the area was here by virtue of his specially issued Phase 4 pass, and the team chiefs had put on their fireproof and blast-proof helmets, each with a bright color easy to distinguish in an emergency.

Near the gantry two men stood talking quietly: the trials control officer and Dr. Chapel, both helmeted. The area ops officer was supervising the fueling. The big HTP/Zenox tanker was already lined up at the aft end of the transporter, the fueling-team dressed in white protective clothing and masks. Three fire tenders were disposed in their strategic alert sectors, their red paint bright in the sunshine. Two ambulances stood by with their rear doors locked open, staffed by first-aid men and nurses. The mobile operating theater was nearby, in the charge of an establishment surgeon trained in emergency work.

The G.S.O. went over and spoke to the fire chief and then looked across at Dr. Chapel, who nodded.

The blanking caps came off the fuel unions and the flexible conduits were swung out from the pumps. The operation was begun.

HTP/Zenox was a fuel that had not yet propelled a missile. It had been static-fired several hundred times in varying conditions and had undergone limit-stress safety checks in the laboratory and the open air. Small quantities of it had been deliberately exploded by "accidental" decomposition, and these experiments had revealed a violently unstable character. Even as a liquid it must not touch the human body and was dangerous to man. As an explosive its potential danger was lethal and massive. It could be handled only in surgically clean conditions and by personnel with six months' rigorous training in the laboratory on the characteristics of this fuel alone. Decomposition could occur by contamination with very simple substances whose electrochemical makeup was interreactive: a splinter of dry wood, a shred of rubber, an oily rag. An HTP/Zenox fire could not be put out by ordinary means; an actual explosion of one tankerful would cover a lethal blast area of three hundred yards' radius. HTP/Zenox was infinitely more dangerous than simple HTP; it was also more powerful under control.

An ugly chemical, it had a potency that made it at once highly attractive to rocket engineers. It had thus been refined, explored, measured, and tested exhaustively until the margin of risk was forced sufficiently narrow to pass the most stringent safety requirements. There was an area in which

HTP/Zenox had not been examined: in actual flight conditions. This had simply not been possible. Its reactions to certain chemicals and electrical phenomena were still unknown, because these chemicals were produced by mutations and these phenomena set up by fluxes experienced only in actual flight conditions at great altitude, which were impossible to simulate in a vacuum chamber.

The risk to the Tokariji establishment was therefore doubled. A partly untried fuel was to power a partly untried missile. But the risk had been shifted into the atmosphere, into the area of conditions unexaminable on the earth's surface. If anything went wrong it was almost a hundred per cent certain that it would go wrong at altitude, at a safe distance from the island.

Chapel had been aware of the HTP/Zenox character. He had left it to the chemists to tame the new fuel if it could be done. His only interest was in that the constituent Zenox, added to High-test Peroxide, gave an ultralow molecular weight to the exhaust gases, an ultrahigh heat release, and therefore 1.9 times the power of simple HTP. The moment the safety authorities had shown their satisfaction in the margin, Chapel had said: "Then we will use this fuel and build an engine to suit it."

The engine was named Theta-Z, being in the Theta series contracted for with Wymark-Vincent. The Z stood for Zenox. In rocketry circles it was more usually known as the Chapel.

Fueling began at 13.20 hours.

It was similar in major respects to a blood transfusion. As the Diesel pumps fed the fuel through the conduits, clinical conditions were maintained. With the passage of every second, measurements were made by a battery of instruments and operators: the levels inside the tanker, exchange reservoirs, and missile tanks; the temperature of the fuel in all branches of the pumping system; the humidity, pressures, and gravities of every "wet" lock and chamber.

These measurements, visible on the dials of the gauges, were collated by computer and announced verbally on the No. 1 Area loudspeaker system so that if there were any discrepancy in the procedure it could be stopped immediately by the fueling-team chief or the ground safety officer or Dr. Chapel.

The wind had died away, true to the Met. report. Above the tanker the canvas shade was motionless now. The sun struck gold from a blue sky and the colored helmets bloomed like strange mushrooms against the dun-brown gantry apron. By 14.05 hours half the fuel had been pumped into the missile.

The resemblance to a blood transfusion was apt in another way. White Lance, cradled horizontally, was still a fragile shell incapable of supporting its own weight. When the fuel was in the tanks and sealed under pressure the missile would have the strength to resist the strains of handling and could be hoisted into the gantry.

"Limits 10, margin point 133."

Irving listened to the computed analysis and watched people's hands and people's faces. The pumping engine throbbed, its exhaust gas led through a twenty-yard pipe clear of the area.

"Limits 11, margin point 139."

Nobody worried. The risk had worsened by six thousandths of a unit, but then it must. The more fuel, the more risk. Only if the safety margin of point 2 were reached would they have to stop pumping.

By 15.10 hours ninety per cent of the fuel was in the missile's tanks.

The sun burned down. Men shifted their feet. Nobody talked.

"Limits 19, margin point 186."

The last gallon went in at 15.23 hours with .009 still left of the margin.

Most of the operators were showing reaction; the shine of sweat was on their faces. Irving's skin was completely dry; he held his position because on his selection-board records it was noted that he functioned psychologically at his best in conditions of hazard.

By 15.35 hours the empty tanker had been driven away from the area, and by the evening of that day White Lance stood erect.

Chapter 14

An hour ago the main lamps had gone out and now the island lay under moonlight, becalmed in the dark sea. It had become ancient again. Formed in the immeasurable ages before man had come, it would be here when man had gone. Man had less permanence than rock.

The surf broke under the moon, ringing the island with white. Here and there a dark outcrop rose from the flatness, held like the head of a mastodon left stranded from times long gone away. It was illusion. Man was here with his contemporary shapes.

Tallest of these by far was the towering skeleton of the gantry, topped by ruby lamps. At this shrine was worshiped no new god, for all its strangeness on such an ancient rock; man had always been devotional in the exploration of his own condition, and now the computer was his rosary.

The tower leaned between earth and moon. Beneath it stood the man. He had come here alone and to be alone. There were men and guard dogs not far away and they watched him but let him be. He was highest in the land.

So all was well. White Lance stood erect. All was well, so far. (The bitter little voice was ever quick to warn him. *So far . . . so far.*)

This far, then, nothing had stopped them. Nothing. One or two of the men had disaffected, unequal to the strain.

Let them go, then, damn them, they were dangerous. Nothing must touch White Lance without love, without understanding of all he was.

He would talk to them, all of them, as soon as he could, and tell them that all was well and would go well with all of them. (His eyelids met together and the scene went dark. Yes, he was tired. Yes, Dr. Friedmann, I'm tired, and I don't need you to tell me.)

Look up again. Tall, slender, shining . . . not yet born, you could say, not yet alive, but already leaping for the stars. Half as high again, dear God! Beyond the ionosphere . . . *Would I could go with you.*

He moved so suddenly that one of the Alsatians gave a bark and the guard spoke a word to quiet it.

He moved before he knew it, pacing deliberately among the shadows of the trellis, because to be motionless was somehow to invite the onset of those thoughts he was best rid of. For instance: *would I could go with you.* White Lance was going to his death.

Better face it. You haven't felt like this since you went out of St. Helen's, down all those steps you counted, one for a blessing, one for a sin, all the way down to the street where people walked as they walk in any town, London or Hiroshima. I must buy some toothpaste—and the next moment their shadow was burned into the stones by the brilliant megatonic light.

But you were not *personally* responsible, they had told him at St. Helen's. You must rid yourself of this feeling that you were *personally* responsible. We all are, come to that.

If you hadn't done that particular work, Jim, someone else would have.

Yes. But it was me.

Let's not start all that again. No black thoughts, now. But my good Dr. Friedmann you seem to be dropping in at my house more frequently these days, on the pretext of discussing the morale of the personnel, and I'll thank you to leave me to fight my own battles, it's the only way.

A dog barked again and he thought: Good dog. Any creature, man, dog, angel, or devil, who safeguarded White Lance was good. Theirs was the only good.

The malaise had passed. The deliberate movement had brought him safely away from the edge of dark, and he could think constructively. He must see Hurst. What had he discovered about the second reconnaissance aircraft? Had he reported to London and what did London say? There must be something more definite too about the keys: had they been taken away or simply been lost?

London would have the final say, damn them. *In requesting these special facilities we are of course fully aware of your personal views on such a situation, but feel sure you will accept it as our confidence in your conviction that the defense of this country takes precedence over every other consideration.*

It had been blackmail, of course, and he shouldn't have let them get away with it, wheeling in a Trojan horse right under his nose.

London, beware. Don't go shopping too lightheartedly for toothpaste.

The trellis of the gantry made a pattern of shadow on the ground that distracted him, so complex was it, and the problem came back to his mind: the design for the autopilot bending stability had been in the most difficult problem area, and three modifications had been carried out, since the factor was threefold. 1) The bending mode frequencies were low, even for third-curve modes. 2) Account had to be taken of at least three modes. 3) The modes were lightly damped, the lowest within 0.5 to 1 per centum. The strategies for the solution had been elegant, and Phil Whymlett—who knew a little about this sphere—had congratulated him. A careful choice of a rate gyro location had provided a zero feedback, using an antimode of slope. Analysis had warned that for higher frequency modes the phase lag of the loop component would increase through 180 degrees; but the choice of gyro location had been wide, and they had almost sauntered through the prime area like dandies choosing a flower. For some of them it had been a demonstration of the value of elegance.

For most of them it had seemed, except for the fascination of the problem per se, an unnecessary exercise. Follett had called it "two days wasted at a time when minutes count." They failed to understand. They had become alien to him, and that was why he had wanted to stand here and look up at the gantry and see White Lance, alone and unsharing with other eyes, and know that he saw perfection.

A dog made a sound and the guard touched it for silence, looking across the moonlit terrain at the man who stood in the shadows of the gantry. You'd know that figure anywhere, jerking along in straight lines and stopping suddenly, hands digging about in the jacket pockets, the light catching the glasses. Usually alone, these days, just as he was now.

The head of the dog swung sharply and he touched it again. Another guard was coming for a word, bored as himself. They stood side by side, watching the small figure in the shadows of the gantry. The air was still and they spoke in whispers.

"That the P.O.?"

"Yes."

"What's his trouble, then?"

"He's only having a look at the Lance." He kept his hand on the dog's rough head, and the tail wagged slowly. "It's the only friend he's got."

Dr. Friedmann sometimes walked to the end of the harbor when his day was over and sat on the warm stones below the light. Watching the rim of the ocean and the sky of stars he would gain a sense of proportion, emptying his mind and then letting the problems fly in again to pasture on fresh ground. Often the trick worked well but there was no luck tonight. He had to go through the whole thing again as a chain of rational concepts, and the answer wouldn't come up. Except that there seemed to be an *influence*.

Something—some one thing—was affecting Tokariji. He couldn't yet see its shape. He was like an astronomer whose calculations pointed to a new star whose unseen presence was affecting the gravitational pull of known neighboring stars; until the telescope picked it up, all that could be seen were its effects. Friedmann's sphere of enquiry was similar, and the psychological affectations on Tokariji were these:

Dr. Chapel was pushing himself too fiercely, but not *only* at the dictates of his deep motivational drives (basically the elemental fear that the phallic missile would fail and prove him impotent). There was something else affecting him.

The personnel were suffering directly under the harshness of his disciplines and their growing doubts of his stability. This afternoon Friedmann had heard a man say: "You know something? Chapel's going quietly round the bend." In addition they were overtaxing their resources through the increasing demand for concentration, and accident proneness was already on the rampage. But there might be nothing alien here—no influential affection at work.

Chapel's now manifest tendency to instability was obviously due in part (greater or smaller?) to the presence on the island of the army unit. Chapel's loathing of war (buried guilt because of his work on the Hiroshima bomb) was well known. St. Helen's had done no more than patch him up—he'd refused further treatment after two months. Yet this answer seemed too easy, or—if germane—inadequate. The "influence" seemed to be at work again here.

Then there was the unpleasant feeling about security. Two visits from unidentified reconnaissance planes, keys missing, and some kind of row between Hurst and Colonel Pyne. (He hadn't been able to track that one to any reliable source, and it remained a subject of rumor.) There was also a hint of dissonance in the Chapel-Hurst relationship, also hard to track down but not dismissible for that. Hurst was a good security man; apart from less abstract indications, his unpopularity was a good enough guide—a first-class snooper found few open doors. Certainly he was a power seeker (poor luck with women, or dominant mother?) and hoarded information like a miser (power over poverty—but in what terms?), but his regard for Chapel as principal officer was exemplary and they'd never appeared to cross swords until lately. No possible answer to this one—lack of data. Unless it was the "influence" at work again.

Mrs. Chapel. Believed herself to be unloved. Not true, but just as affective. And of course frustrated. These factors had little bearing, however cruel they were to her personally. No "influence." Even Chapel himself not affected: his whole psyche was occupied with White Lance, the representative of all subliminal drives.

Friedmann sat for another hour on the warm stones, trying the trick again, watching the moon's path shifting on the water and listening to the silence out there, letting his mind be led away and then whipping suddenly back on the problem as a cat pounces after a show of disinterest—and there was no luck, no answer. There was an influence directly affecting the whole of the island, but he couldn't name it.

Walking back from the harbor through the shadows between the lamps he chanced to kick against a stone and heard it clattering away, and later looked back on this night to remember the stone he had touched but had never seen, had never recognized.

There were few people about, and voices were faint on the air. A sickness had come to Tokariji. They were taking the strain but they couldn't take it forever. Something must break.

Looking back, later, on the night of the stone, he did not reproach himself for lack of perception; there was no evidence that the first to break would be Colonel Pyne.

Chapter 15

There were two ways of reaching the Telex hut from the army quarters and the distance was much the same. Major Nash took the path that led between the Chapels' house and the guesthouse, because it was there that he'd had the luck to meet Mrs. Chapel, quite by chance, the other night. So if he met her now it wouldn't be by chance, and he knew this very well and was a fraction bothered by it.

There was no future, of course. Eve was a married woman. It was better to forget her. The trouble was that he couldn't. It had got to the stage where it was putting him off his food. He'd almost mentioned it to Ken once or twice but couldn't quite screw up the courage. Brother officers were meant to take their troubles to one another if they got in a stew, and the C.O. of any unit was father to his flock and all that. But Ken was an older man and a damned sight more experienced; he'd probably laugh at him, or want to, and not, which would be worse. And even in his current mood of gay defiance or whatever it was, you couldn't get inside those defenses. This had to be weathered alone.

After a dozen yards he turned back and started along the other path, where he was less likely to meet her. On the other hand he might see her anywhere—she went all over the place. The Chapels' house was still not far away; he could see the lamp on the veranda from here. Certainly you'd never notice it unless you were looking for it. Let's face it: he was looking for it.

There were some people—two men and a woman—coming up from the civilian living quarters on their way to the senior mess, and the woman looked very suntanned in the faint light, so he just turned round and went back to the Nissens and began on the first path again, sweating like mad and very angry, God knew who with. Then he heard the woman laugh quietly on the other side of the tamarisk hedge, and it wasn't Eve's laugh at all, much less delightful.

He kept straight on. It was in any case damned silly to take all this trouble trying to avoid her, when the next time he walked into the mess she'd more than likely be there—she often was. Then he'd have to speak to her. Better to steer clear of the mess, really.

Damn it all, he wasn't going to confine himself to camp!

Mind over matter. Robert Nash, you are an officer and a gentleman, and crazy about a girl who is the lawful wedded wife of a most respected boffin who happens also, in a way, to be your host. So bloody well forget it, the whole thing. Not that there's anything to bloody well remember, worse luck.

He arrived at the Telex hut exhausted.

Over the doorway was a crudely painted board: HEAD OFFICE—THE TOKA TIMES. Some wag. But the news was pukka all right, coming through the main agencies, and it was his job to get it typed up and put on the board for the boys every day.

He took a different path back, met no one, and was heartily glad and bitterly sorry. Sergeant Lacey was still on duty in the C.O.'s office, and he stayed to help him get the news typed up, dictating it straight on to a machine. It was mostly about Malaysia again.

Britain went into action this morning with a concerted series of moves giving Malaysian defenses support against the threat of powerful attacks by the Indonesian forces, which are equipped with Soviet-built warships and submarines. Two

*of our parachute battalions have left England for Singapore,
while troopships ply between Singapore and Malaysian Borneo to aid the work of reactivating the Far Eastern Fleet.
The whole situation is becoming increasingly serious, and
several spokesmen are unofficially admitting: "It could be another Cuba."*

*Behind the scene looms Communist China, who is expected
to have the means, within a few years, of launching short-range nuclear missiles. Against this threat is the announcement that the United States Government is "fully prepared
to deploy the new A5 submarine-based missile in any area
where world peace is seen to be threatened."*

Sergeant Lacey spun the platen and spread out the three
duplicates for correction.

"No wonder they sent us out here with a Triton."

Nash told him firmly: "We are here for training."

"Yes, sir. I clean forgot."

"Don't forget again, especially in front of the men."

He left the office, annoyed. It seemed clear that the unit
was here to await possible orders for a fast shift to a Far East
operational area in an emergency, where they could use their
Javelin 33s effectively. Certainly their training with the unarmed Triton was a genuine fact, and they were already becoming proficient in the early-alert drill. To question the official reason for their presence on Tokariji was to risk the
starting of false rumors, and that was a point on which the
C.O. was particularly hot.

He was halfway to the senior mess when it occurred to him
that she might be there and that he might have to speak to
her. All right, it would force him to prove his new resolve
and treat her as what she was: the respected wife of his civilian host. He would even start calling her "Mrs. Chapel"
again to show her that things had changed between them and
must stay that way.

Eve was such a wonderful name.

No half-measures, you fool. You'll drive yourself up the

wall. Just greet her respectfully—"Good evening, Mrs. Chapel"—and take it from there. Be brave, and it won't hurt too much.

He walked into the mess as if he'd kicked the door down, a grenade in each hand with the pin out.

There wasn't a woman in sight. Two civilians broke off their talk at the bar, looking alarmed. He composed his face.

"'Evening, Major."

"A double. Good evening."

"Double Scotch?"

"Yes."

He took it down the long room, seeing Wilson and Stoner at a table in one of the alcoves. It would be good to talk to them, it didn't matter a damn what about.

He came round the partition and saw that Ken was there, too, and saw that Ken was drunk.

Wilson pushed a spare chair for him and he sat down, noting that the bottle on the table was down to less than a quarter. Wilson looked all right; so did Stoner; so did Ken, really; a stranger would have called him sober. You had to know him. The amber eyes were a shade narrowed; the attitude was a degree arrogant—one leg bent under the chair and the other stretched out in the pose of an indulgent Caesar; the head was tilted, ready for amusement.

"My good Robert, you're late in the field." The tone of a sleepy lion. "You have thus lost valuable ground." He lifted the bottle with a perfectly sure hand, adding to Nash's whisky. "In what climes have you been disporting your goodself, while we've been here campaigning?"

Nash took up his glass and they all said cheers.

"I've been down to the Telex. Gave Lacey a hand typing it up."

"And what is the word from Delphi?"

"Malaysia, mostly. Things seem to be blowing up there into a full-scale war. Some bright spokesman calls it another—"

Ken's hand hit the bottle and it smashed against the wall with the explosion of a small bomb. Splinters of glass flashed back across the table. A hiss of shock came from Stoner. Nash looked up into Ken's face—he was now on his feet—and hardly recognized it. The teeth were bared and the eyes burning.

After the crash of glass the whole room had gone deathly quiet. The words came slowly, each spoken with force.

"You will in future . . . refrain from speaking of war . . . in my presence."

His chair grated. They stood up and watched him walk, erect and in good order, to the door. It slammed behind him.

A few seconds passed, then Wilson murmured quickly: "What do we do?"

Nash said: "Sit down again." He didn't know if it were the right decision but it was a decision. They sat down awkwardly.

One of the civilians at the bar gave a short laugh. "We-ell . . . bloody hell!"

Nash picked up his glass. "Drink," he murmured. Wilson and Stoner obeyed at once. Every civilian in the room was watching them. Nash tried to sit at his ease, idly flicking the glass fragments into a central pile, saying to Stoner without looking at him: "Dab your face."

Stoner pressed his handkerchief to his temple and the blood soaked into it. "Sorry. Ricochet." He managed a cheerful smile.

"Shouldn't we go?" asked Wilson quietly. He felt a bit daft, sitting here among all the broken glass as if nothing had happened.

"We'll go when we've finished our drink," Nash said.

His glass had been topped up to nearly half, and when Ken had done it he'd thought: "I don't have to drink it all, just make a show." Now, what with one thing and another, he was going to knock off the lot. He thought: "Thank God Eve wasn't here."

The civilians were talking again and being decent enough to get into the act and pretend nothing had happened.

Nash said: "Just tell me what you were talking about, before I showed up, will you?"

"Christ," said Stoner, "nothing special. Nothing important." He looked at Wilson. "Was it?"

"Oh come on," Nash said. "What got him to that pitch?"

"I quite honestly can't think, Bob. He was just in the mood for a blind, and we decided to sit it out with him, knowing it wouldn't show." He dabbed his temple again.

"Not much," said Wilson, rather strained. The bottle effort hadn't been so bad; it was the look of Ken's face just afterward.

"Something must have got him like that," said Nash. But he knew with sudden intuition that it needn't necessarily have been anything they'd been talking about. You couldn't ever get through that man's defenses, but now he had come crashing through them himself, and for the first time they had seen his face, the one that had been inside there all the time.

"It was you," Wilson said, "who made him blow up. Mentioning war. He said as much."

Nash flicked the last fragment of glass against the heap. The stain was still spreading on the plasterboard wall. "It doesn't make sense. That's what we exist for, isn't it? The risk of war?"

Then they heard the door open and saw Sergeant Lacey looking around. The civilians had stopped talking again. The three officers sat waiting. The sergeant saw them and came smartly across—one, two, one, two, one, two—halt. Salute.

You could always rely, thought Nash obliquely, on Lacey putting up a brisk show in public, just as you could rely on the C.O. to walk steadily, however drunk, however agonized.

"Permission to speak, sir?"

"Yes, Lacey."

"Commanding officer's compliments, sir, and he'd like to

see you immediately." He had glanced once at the glass on the table, once at the stain on the wall. His expression remained set.

Nash got up, murmuring to Wilson and Stoner: "Company to retire in good order." Their feet sounded very loud across the quiet room. He gave the barman a pound note. "There's been some damage. If it comes to more than that, please let me know."

They went out in single file, the sergeant bringing up the rear and shutting the door without a sound. Nash told his brother officers: "Drop in at my room. We may want to talk later."

He walked with Sergeant Lacey along the tamarisk hedge. The moonlight threw clear-cut shadows.

"Mr. Pyne simply sent for me, did he? Didn't say anything else?"

"No, sir." There was in Lacey's voice the unease that his face didn't show. He kept punctiliously in step.

"Where is he?"

"He said he'd be in his room, sir."

Nash walked quickly, forcing himself along, wanting to run in the opposite direction. He had never feared men's rage, knowing it for childishness; but he was a coward when it came to watching pain in others; and tonight Ken was in worse pain than he'd ever seen in a man.

He dismissed Lacey at the first Nissen and went on alone.

The C.O. answered to his second knock. He was standing precisely in the middle of his room, subconsciously expressing his need to retain command from the center. He was standing correctly at ease and his cap was still on. Nash shut the door and came to attention.

He looked at Ken's face and knew that he mustn't show pity or he'd get half-killed for it. Ken had once told him: "Your weakest point is your sense of pity. You'd do well to get rid of it."

He said now: "Please be at your ease, Robert." He turned

away and stood facing the window, and Nash heard with every word that he was stone cold sober; his will had simply rejected the influence of the alcohol. Later he might yield again, and be drunk again, and it would probably—thought Nash—be good for him.

"I owe you an explanation."

The word was carefully chosen. There would be no apology. Ken never apologized.

"You, and Stoner, and Wilson. But my explanation can be made to you alone, for reasons of security. My express orders are to withhold certain information from the entire company, the adjutant included. I have decided to disobey those orders and pass on this information to you. Your good sense, and your good will toward me, which I greatly prize, are my surety that you will keep this information strictly to yourself."

Some ten or twelve seconds passed. Nash listened to the tick of the bedside clock. He wanted to move his feet, shove his hands in his pockets, make any small action to break this dreadful silence; but he stood steady.

"The information was received by coded cable on the night when we were invited to dine at the Chapels' house. Since that time it has burdened me, Robert. You will have noticed certain regrettable changes in what I hope might be called my normal good spirits, since that time. I found it difficult to keep this matter to myself. I managed, until now."

It was said without satisfaction, without any feeling at all in his tone. The words were spoken out of a face that itself showed nothing except that the mind was numbed.

"In deliberately flouting orders I am acting on my own instincts. It seems to me that if I ask you to share this burden there's a good chance that I shall repair my spirit and be able to retain command of this well-loved company of men whose respect is my greatest need, however little I sometimes appear to earn it. It's not my wish to go to pieces in front of such men, as I did tonight in front of my officers. But that might well happen, if I don't seek your support."

Silence began again and then he turned suddenly to face Nash, startling him. "You're younger than I am, Robert. How old are you? I've never asked."

"Thirty-one, sir."

The amber eyes considered. An expression had crept into them but Nash couldn't name it; perhaps it was envy of a kind.

"Thirty-one. Then I've had sixteen more years in which to think. When I was your age I was probably more of your mind—we're soldiers, aren't we, then let's have a lovely war! Isn't that what we're for?" He braced his shoulders; they had been drooping by an inch. "But the concept of war is different in these days. We shan't aim at the railheads or the ammunition dumps or the pocket across the hill. We shall be committed to the obliteration of capitals."

He swung his head, as if hearing something. Nash had heard nothing. The eyes in the drawn face came back to rest on him.

"I will get to business, Robert. We are not here for training. We are here on general-alert standby. We have already learned to fire the Triton; it can be aimed, triggered, and fired within the required twenty-three minutes. And this is my worry. This is my worry. I've disobeyed orders, in telling you this. What a man does he may do again. I don't know, if I receive orders to fire the Triton, whether I shall obey. That isn't a new solid-fuel motor under guard in the blockhouse; it's a thousand-megaton nuclear warhead, and the target is the city of Peking."

Chapter 16

The silence of the Tokariji night is so profound that one must stop and let the ear absorb it, as one must stop and let the eye absorb a great view from a high place.

Nash had paused twice to experience the soundlessness that surrounded him, once outside his quarters, which he had left as stealthily as a thief so as to wake no one, and again on the south rim of the weapon pit, where he had wandered in order to think. He had been in many places alone by night, and knew the difference in this one. There was no grass on Tokariji, and scant foliage; thus there were no insects or birds or mammals here; the place was a dead rock. Tonight there was no breeze; the sea, too, was dead. There was only the moon, as dead as the rock and the sea. Stoner and Wilson had been waiting in his room as he asked them, and he had told them the half-truth that the C.O. had agreed to.

"It looks as if things might blow up in Malaysia. If they do, we'll be sent in closer and issued with a warhead, and may get orders to shoot it. Ken's not keen on the idea of blotting out a major town. That's all."

They were quiet for a minute and he was impatient with their disbelief. Wilson said:

"Well, I suppose it's enough."

"He should have talked to me about it before," went on Nash, "or anyone, come to that. But you know Ken; he

142

doesn't easily ask for help. He'll be all right now he's got if off his chest."

He hoped it might be true. Ken had seemed more at ease when he'd left him. They'd even sat down and smoked a cigarette while Ken had filled in the picture for him: "This base was chosen because the best place to hide a missile is among a lot of others, in this case known to be peaceful research vehicles. In the normal way the whole unit would know it had been given a warhead; but this is a civilian base and the risk of the information leaking out is very high. If the population knew there was a thousand-megaton war-head sitting here—big enough to blow the whole island to hell—they'd run us out of the place. Obviously the War Office wants to keep us here, so they minimized the risk by coding the signal and telling me to call the thing a solid-fuel motor."

Nash had asked: "What about if things get hot in Malaysia?"

"We would place Tokariji under immediate military law and arm the Triton." The strain came back to his tone. "It's my hope there'll be no occasion. If it's going to be another Cuba they'll have to work out an answer as they had to before. Let the bloody politicians earn their bread." He got up, walking about angrily. "Let them feel fright for themselves, Robert, this time. In the First World War they sat pretty—they took the butter and gave us the guns. In the second there was more risk because of the bombing. In the third there'll only be one frontline trench, and every man jack of us in it. Let's hope it might make them consider. They're already expressing their pious anxiety at the idea of the world itself laid waste, but it's not the world they think of, it's themselves—their own bald and vulnerable heads. The Somme was a world and so was the Marne and they trod them into the mud. This time it's their world, their wife and their child, and it's got them worried, that. Nationality's lost its meaning at last: this generation has a common birthplace—Hiroshima. It's a place to go carefully in."

He had stopped pacing and looked down at Nash. "It's good to talk to you, Robert. I know you don't see it my way but to hell with that. It's good to say it."

Nash had sat listening, knowing how it healed. The amber eyes had life in them again, even anger; the awful blank look had gone. Ken talked about the reconnaissance plane; it had been the second, apparently, over the island in a matter of weeks. "They may be interested in the civilian project, White Lance, and not us. Or there's been a leak somewhere at home, and someone knows the army's here. Or there's been a leak here, I don't know. The point is, it isn't the time to let anyone know what we've got in the woodshed, Robert."

"You've given me an order, and you've got my word." He had managed a smile. "Double insurance."

"Oh, I'm not drumming it in. Just talking. Not often I talk, is it? Good medicine."

Then he had closed up again and his tone was once more colorless. "As a British missile unit we form a very small part of the unilateral defense plan. Last year the United States deployed a squadron of B52 heavy jet nuclear bombers on Guam Island, at two thousand miles' range of Communist China—the closest they've been. Each aircraft carries two twenty-four-megaton bombs, the equivalent of close to fifty million tons of TNT per aircraft. Since then the ring around China has been drawn tighter, and our unit based on Tokariji is now a link in the chain of ICBM missile posts. So we're not alone."

His mouth had tightened. "Let the thought console us and give us comfort: as an instrument of wholesale death, we are not alone."

When Nash had left him he had been standing as before, in the middle of the room, but his cap had been thrown onto a chair and his arms were folded; he looked no more than desperately tired.

There was nothing else to tell Wilson and Stoner. They didn't understand; they would just have to accept the explanation.

"Of course," Wilson told Nash after a moment, "I don't really get it, but since you say so . . ."

"We've got to revise our ideas about Ken, is all I know." He oughtn't to feel so annoyed with their lack of understanding. They'd understand better if they knew what was in that bloody woodshed.

"I knew a bloke," said Stoner quietly, "in the war. He was trained as a bomb-aimer and passed out best of his bunch. First time up, over the target, he reported the bomb doors were jammed, so they came back with a full load. Got out of the plane and went straight to the squadron doctor, told him cheerfully that he'd gone round the bend and wouldn't be coming back. The bomb doors hadn't jammed—he'd seen the town below him and couldn't pull that fucking lever, not for king, country, or Jesus Christ —and never would. Finished up as a clock repairer, got a small shop in the Strand. Parallel case, I suppose. Ken any good at clocks?"

Nash was grateful to him; the story could even be true.

"Takes all sorts," said Wilson, and left it at that. Before they went, Nash said:

"We don't have to get this thing out of proportion. Ken had a worry on his mind, and now he's trotted it out. He'll be more his old self in future. Okay?"

Walking alone now in the light of the moon with the dark weapon pit below him, he knew it wasn't true. Ken had no "old self" to go back to; he had never been the man they thought they'd known. A few things, though, were clearer now to Nash; one was the C.O.'s mood of gay defiance that had followed the earlier sourness. Shocked by the coded signal, he had felt himself cut off from the unit because he couldn't share the news; he was ordered to lie to the men whose respect was precious to him; and the estrangement got on his nerves until the day when he worked out a new attitude, which was: All right, we're soldiers and we've got a job to do; if the order comes to blow up the world there's only one answer. Salute and press the tit.

That attitude had sustained him for a time, but it was against his nature, and the mask had slipped and the bottle had smashed and there had stood Ken in his true colors, a man of whom you could ask too much, soldier or no.

The moon threw clear shadows and the pit was dark as Nash wandered along its rim. The silence unnerved him. If the final orders ever came, they wouldn't be alone in what they had to do, and afterward this lifeless silence would be everywhere.

"*Who goes there?*"

The shout startled him and he cursed aloud. It was the corporal of the guard.

"Friend!" he answered into the dark pit.

"Advance, friend, and be recognized!"

He moved to the very edge. "I can't, without breaking my bloody neck."

A beam of light struck him full in the eyes and he suffered it while the corporal satisfied himself; then it dulled out.

"I didn't know who it was, sir." There was smugness in the man's tone; he thought Nash was making a snap check to see if the guard was alert.

"All well, Corporal?"

"All's well, sir."

Nash turned and made his way back toward the huts, his nerves still unsettled. Three men, alone in the mid-ocean night, stood guard at the gates of a city three thousand miles away where five million people lived and, if the order came, would die.

"The concept of war is different in these days," Ken had told him.

He thought: "I understand."

Pyne did not sleep; it was too quiet tonight, and even the surf's distant sound was missing. One could sleep in the din of a city and in the drum of bombardment, but in stillness such as this one's thoughts were louder than either.

He heard Nash moving in the adjoining room, and from the window saw him take the path toward the weapon pit. Poor Robert. He'd taken the news hard and couldn't sleep himself; he was going to check the guard on the blockhouse because now he knew what was there.

Pyne watched him until he passed into shadows. Should he go out and catch him up? They could talk again. But no; he'd done enough talking; it was good medicine but repeated doses would be habit-forming, and there was this thing on his mind that could never be talked about, even to Robert, especially to Robert. He didn't want to see contempt on Robert's face.

God had given man a brain to think with and a heart to love with and—to drive him mad—a conscience.

He stood at the open window. The silence was absolute; the ears sang with it. Sound was a part of life; people and objects were linked together by it into known patterns; you could shut your eyes and still know that life went on in the world around. Here on this rock, this mid-ocean mountain peak beleaguered by the dark, there was no more sound; life was no more linked; the known patterns had gone. The supports had been knocked away and you could believe that at any instant the moon could fall into the sea and your body into the earth forever.

Not a bad thing.

Who would worry, who would know? Not Margaret. Where was she now? *Let's look at it squarely, Ken. We've come unstuck. We eat together and sleep together but we go on being strangers. We can't talk to each other. There's no—well—touchstone. Is inarticulateness a grounds for divorce? Two complete strangers have slept together for three years; that ought to be sinful enough for the court.*

Sorry, old boy, but it's come to that. I can't stand it, and nor can you.

What sort of weakness or vice was it in a man that he couldn't talk to other men, to women? Fear of what? Of being known too well by his words? What then was so unknowable about him that others would look away if they saw it? Or was it that there was *nothing* to know, nothing to tell, nothing to show but a thing as dull as a stone? A bore.

Faintly he heard across the moonlight: *"Halt! Who goes there?"*

Yes, checking the guard.

Murmuring; then the silence returned.

This was an island silence. More than profound, it was isolated, insulated. *Insula:* an island. One was cut off. The world had shrunk to a rock. One had lost proportion, perspective. Caged claustrophobically with that Satan-black inmate of the blockhouse, one had to live with it; the thing was thrust on one's company; it thus assumed too great an importance. People too were thrust on one, and there was no room here to stand back; the closeness made false giants of them; Chapel . . . Hurst . . . others.

Men should not have to live together in so small a cage. It was not civilized. It made one do undreamed of things.

Cold fact: they were done, and no going back.

A figure was dark in the moonlight suddenly and passed close by the window, and a door closed softly.

Sleep, my good Robert, if you can. And don't blame me too much.

Chapter 17

It was getting so bad now that Phil Whymlett found himself thinking of excuses not to go to the Chapels' house. At first he thought these excuses were genuine, but as soon as he knew it was self-deception he felt angry and called himself a coward.

Evie and Jim needed help and he could give it, if only by sharing their disharmony. There were no scenes; it was worse than that—their very politeness to each other was chilling to listen to. On some nights, to avoid the strained intimacy of the dinner table, he took a cold chicken along from the communal store, and a bottle of wine—"We'll hack it to pieces on the veranda, picnic-style, and watch the moon come up." They lit the two lamps outside; there were no insects on Tokariji.

His best chance of helping them was when he found Evie alone, before Jim came across from his office, and was able to put Jim's point of view to her as Jim himself could not. It was so obvious but it seemed it needed saying:

"We're going into Phase 5 tomorrow, Evie. Tomorrow we static-fire White Lance in the launcher and you know what that means; it's the most dangerous part of the whole sequence, more so than even the final blast-off, because the missile stays on the ground the whole time until the tanks are empty. So is it surprising that Jim's on edge? We all are! It's been a long haul, Evie—six weeks, and two to go. There are people being taken off work every day because the pace is too much for them, and the fresh replacements are taking over. Area 1 has become a kind of front line; the wounded are being withdrawn and the reserves sent in." He lowered his voice. "There's no reserve for Jim."

She watched his face in the lamplight, not interrupting because she knew he wanted to talk, to tell himself these things; Phil was feeling the strain as much as anyone else and believed he didn't show it. His broad and rather lumpy face had a permanent frown; his hands were never still.

But sometimes she, too, had to say things, because there was nobody else to tell. One night while they were waiting for Jim she shocked him: it hadn't been meant to shock him, but it couldn't be unsaid. He had been talking about White Lance.

"There has never been a missile like it, Evie. In a year from now you'll look back on these nervy times and see that we've all made history. There are steps in space research that become landmarks, and—"

"I'm tired of missiles," she said very low.

He took it like a blow on the face and she regretted it at once but couldn't stop. "And I'm sorry for White Lance. This won't be easy for you to believe: White Lance has become human to me. Not human, then, but animal—just something alive. It has a beautiful shape, especially with the sun on it. You and Jim and the others are creating something beautiful, and soon you'll kill it. Only rationalizing makes it seem otherwise. A shoot is an act of calculated destruction, an execution. And there's something morbid about the intense care that you give to everything you do."

"But *Evie* . . ."

"Oh, I know. Consciously you're conducting an experiment; it's not the missile you're concerned with—that's doomed from the start. It's scientific data you need; you're analyzing space. But subconsciously you're preparing a sacrifice for the scaffold, and when it's been duly and ritually done to death you'll make the autopsy. Then you'll be satisfied; I don't like to think in what way."

Her voice had risen and when she finished there was no quick smile; she wasn't even looking at him.

"It's a . . . fanciful point of view, Evie." It was the most he wanted to answer. He was here to help, not make things worse. Besides, however fanciful she was being, he often heard remarks these days among the technicians that made him pause. Superstition was being voiced without intention, by men who were feeling the strain more than others; even their behavior showed it: yesterday he had seen a man walk under a ladder and turn back and walk under it again and go round it. Someone had said: "Don't worry. The night we shoot, everything'll go like clockwork—tick-tick-tick-Tokariji!" The nearest piece of wood he could find was halfway down the test shop and he had walked there and back to touch it, and nothing would have stopped him. Uncertain of their science, they were seeking the help of gods. He remembered now, especially, something a man said only this morning, after a tense two-hour struggle with a fail-safe installation. "It's bloody odd, you know, the trouble we're taking to kill a cock just so we can study the entrails."

Evie had called it an autopsy after a ritual killing.

She was speaking again and he watched her as she leaned closer to him, urging him to understand, speaking now about Jim and perhaps hurrying in case he should come and overhear. "Jim had a breakdown, once. Did you know?"

"St. Helen's."

"Yes. And I'm afraid for him now. I'm afraid what White Lance can do to him. I don't know what will happen if this shoot fails—I mean happen to Jim. I'm going to be fanciful again: a missile is armed with the means of its own destruction, isn't it? I'm afraid he is, too. A lot of people are."

He thought about that while she sat silent. No, it wasn't so fanciful. It just didn't have to be thought about. And there was no real answer. He said:

"It's no good saying people oughtn't to climb mountains, Evie."

Then Jim came along the path by the tamarisk hedge and they hacked up the chicken Phil had brought, and he didn't taste it because of what had been said, and told himself he would never bring another damned chicken here again.

On the morning of Day 1, Phase 5, Dr. Chapel found a reminder on his memo pad and sent for the security officer.

In contrast to almost everyone else, Hurst seemed at his ease and confident. It was, Chapel thought, because Hurst had nothing to do with the technical aspect of the shoot and was unconcerned by its mass of problems. On the other hand he had problems of his own, no less acute; White Lance was the subject of fierce security.

"You remember my asking you to find out everything possible, Mr. Hurst, about the appearance of the first reconnaissance aircraft overhead this island, and whether we would have any grounds for suspecting a security leak in the establishment. There has since been a second occurrence, reported by Colonel Pyne, and observed by our instrumentation. There has also been a case of lost keys. May I have your comments?"

Hurst waited before answering. The P.O. had lowered his gaze to some papers on the desk; they were technical drawings. Anything that was said now would not be heard.

In some forty-five seconds Dr. Chapel looked up and Hurst said: "I'll send my reports across as soon as I get back, Dr. Chapel. Meanwhile I can say verbatim that I made very careful enquiries on the recco planes, here and in England. I'm prepared to say the leak—and of course there was a leak—didn't originate from Tokariji."

Chapel studied the round pink face and the shortsighted-looking eyes. "I am impressed."

"Surprised, too. I can see that, sir."

"Yes, I am also surprised. And of course relieved."

"There was a lot of work attached—an immense amount of work. The reports go into quite a few pages and there's a whole batch of interviews on record. If you ever find time to read them you'll see why I can afford to sound so confident. Those keys were a help." He pressed his lips into a bright smile. "We didn't find them, but the enquiry I made was pretty thorough and while I was at it I didn't forget about the recco planes. If the leak had come from here, internally, I would have got on to it, there's no question."

"The keys were a help, Mr. Hurst?"

"Oh yes."

Chapel looked down at the drawings again and a minute went by before he got up and stood with his hands fretting in his jacket pockets. "It has been said that you took the keys yourself, you know."

"Yes, I heard the rumor." He smiled again, his eyes gleaming.

"Did you take them?"

"I don't need to do things like that, Dr. Chapel. If I want to turn the whole establishment upside down and shake it, I don't have to fabricate an excuse. It's my job to poke about, you know that. It's not surprising no one likes me—show me a popular security officer and I'll show you a man who's not doing his job."

The P.O. nodded quickly. "I am sure you are right."

"We still don't know how those keys were lost but it's my opinion it was accidental. Someone didn't want to own up to carelessness, especially to me. The lock was changed and there's been no further instance; not bad, is it, in a place where we've got a hundred and forty-seven sets of keys?"

He watched the P.O. In the last month he'd aged five

years. A lot of them had, but Chapel showed it the most. It was a shame, and Hurst was sorry. He could respect a man who was efficient, who would take his aim and not let anything stop him getting to the goal—even his own peace of mind. People called them ruthless; that was envy. A lot of things were said because of envy. People didn't like you having power, and the reason was the same.

"Then I am satisfied, Mr. Hurst."

"You'll get the reports right away, sir." He paused at the door. "I suppose you've found no good reason yet for inspecting Colonel Pyne's equipment?"

Chapel considered before he answered.

"You may know that security in the services is of as high an order as in civilian quarters and that the two spheres are in close liaison. Why have you no confidence, in this respect, in Colonel Pyne?"

"Oh, I've confidence in his security."

"As you should have." His hands were digging about in his pockets restlessly. "We shall leave it at that, Mr. Hurst."

"If anything comes my way, I'll report to you." He opened the door. He had got what he was after. The P.O. was upset, and it spoke volumes.

When he had gone, Chapel sat down again and turned the technical drawings over so that they shouldn't distract him. His hands remained on the desk, and they trembled a little.

Surely it was impossible that Hurst knew. He himself and Colonel Pyne alone were meant to know. Yet, on the evening when Pyne had come to dinner, neither had known. He had not been informed until the day of its arrival. Presumably Pyne had received a coded signal. There was no code in use by the civilian establishment; a man had simply come to see him. He had flown in with the consignment and was in the uniform of a navigator, but he was not a navigator.

"You received a signal about special cargo, Dr. Chapel?"

"I did."

"It's just landed."

The man had been a very quiet person with steady eyes and a quality of calm in his voice. One trusted him at once, and—worse—one felt open to his least persuasion. He first gave him a letter; it referred to special cargo consigned to the army unit and requested that all facilities be given Colonel Pyne for its handling, if asked for. *In requesting these special facilities we are of course fully aware of your personal views on such a situation but feel sure you will accept it as our confidence in your conviction that the defense of this country takes precedence over every other consideration.*

He had read it twice and was little the wiser.

"What is the nature of this cargo?"

The uniformed man looked at the communicating door. They could hear Mary typing in the other room. Whenever she paused the building was very quiet. The man asked him for the note pad, and tore off the top sheet, laying it on the desk before he wrote, so that the sheet below should carry no impression. He held the paper and let him read. *Nuclear warhead for Triton.* He flicked his cigarette lighter and burned the paper, breaking up the remains in the ashtray.

"No, I cannot allow that!" Chapel stood up, looking around him—the window, the door, the blackboard—perhaps in his panic trying to reorientate himself in his known surroundings because an age had passed since the time when the man had begun writing, and he felt himself to have become lost. Then the man was talking quietly and persuasively, standing up so that they could face each other. He had listened, and a word had got through to him, then another and a third, until he was sitting down again and saying, "I consider it unfair, grossly unfair . . ."

When the man had left him, the thing was done.

He could not even remember his face, only his voice and

his persuasiveness. Who was that man? They must have chosen their best, telling him: "You'll have a hard nut to crack. Chapel's a hundred per cent pacifist. Don't mention Hiroshima to him. Explain the obvious: that the only chance of world survival is in the balance of power—nuclear power. Tell him that in the final game of kill and overkill it's going to be the side with the *hidden* weapons that will come through. Tell him there's no better hiding place than Tokariji—we're putting a tree in a wood."

Perhaps the man had said: "What if he stops the White Lance project or threatens to?" If so, they had told him: "He won't do that . . ."

There had been one solution: to immerse himself in the project, deeply and utterly, and blot out of his mind the black remains in the ashtray.

It had been for the most part possible, except when he had glimpsed the sharp finger of the Triton pointing from the weapon pit, and when Hurst had suggested that he should "inspect" Colonel Pyne's equipment. Now he had mentioned it again, and it had been too dangerous even to ask him why. Had Hurst wondered, on the earlier occasion, why he had refused to support him over the episode in the weapon pit when seemingly Pyne had ordered him out? He surely must have.

Hurst could not possibly *know*. They had been explicit about that. "You and Colonel Pyne," the quiet-voiced man had said, "are the only two people to be given this information. Colonel Pyne has been ordered to withhold it even from his own officers. We shall inform no one else."

Hurst could only suspect. Was that dangerous, even that he suspected, even though he was a security officer?

Suddenly he found that he was sitting with his face buried in his hands and that he was murmuring something over and over again . . . "Not my concern, it is not my concern . . ."

He got up quickly and moved about—to be motionless was to invite the onset of those thoughts he was best rid of. He moved now as he had moved among the trellis shadows of the gantry, reestablishing himself physically, touching the blackboard and the edge of the desk and the windowsill, known things, safe bearings, the pole stars of his black and terror-bringing night.

Then the door opened and Mary was standing there.

"Mary?"

"Yes, Dr. Chapel." Seeing how pale he was, she started forward, then held still.

He looked up at her and for a time said nothing; it was enough to see her there. Known things had not vouchsafed his return to the known world; he had needed suddenly and desperately a known person, and without thinking had pressed the bell. Above all others she was the most known to him.

"Is everything all right?" he asked.

"Yes. Everything is all right." She sounded unsurprised that he had asked; she seemed to understand. The kindness of her voice was healing, and he was able to smile.

"I just wanted to know, Mary."

"Of course, Dr. Chapel."

She closed the door gently and slipped a blank sheet into her typewriter, clicking away at gibberish for a few minutes so that he would hear and be reassured, and so that she would not, in a silent room, give way to sobbing.

Chapter 18

Precisely at 14.00 hours, Day 1, Phase 5, conditions of emergency standby were announced on the public-address network. Thereafter the preliminary Klaxon alerts were sounded at fifteen-minute intervals until 15.00 hours, when the special-duty personnel began leaving Area 1. Ten minutes later the range area was deserted, and White Lance was for the first time in many weeks unattended.

The final warning "Red" was announced and repeated three times.

All personnel not in possession of the Phase 5 pass must remain in the safety sector east of the line from harbor to power station. Any person standing exposed on a rooftop or similar vantage point even in the safety sector will risk his life. We are now operating in conditions of emergency standby and there will be no further verbal warning announced. In a few minutes the final-alert Klaxon will sound.

Irving, ground safety officer, had personally been to see Colonel Pyne, requesting him to withdraw the whole of his unit east of the safety line. He had now come back and was standing on the roof of the Instrumentation Building with his field glasses. The heat haze swam in the lenses. In a moment he called down to the P.A. man:

"There's someone fooling around with a bulldozer near

the airstrip tower. Get him out." He raised the field glasses again, sweeping the terrain.

Special warning. The man with the bulldozer near the airstrip tower is in the danger zone. Until he is on the east side of the safety line we cannot proceed. Timing is vital, and we are waiting for him.

Irving rechecked the area. Within half a minute a trail of sand dust drew out from the control tower as the man flogged his bicycle across the safety line. He would be sweating, Irving knew, not with fear but embarrassment.

He scanned for the last time and went below to join those in the Control Center: the P.O., area ops officer, trials control officer, missile officer, officer in scientific charge. The key men in their teams totaled fifteen. There were now twenty-four people remaining on this side of the east safety line, and they were together in the Control Center.

The only daylight came from the two narrow horizontal prisms, heavily armored and furnished with a steel drop shield that would automatically come down if heat or blast pressure passed the safety limit. Fluorescent tubes glowed along the control and indicator panels.

No one was talking. They had all looked up when the ground safety officer had come in; now they were ready again at the dials. Air pulsed softly through the grills of the conditioner and dust-extraction plants.

It was now that Phil Whymlett, present as an observer of an operation not in his domain, experienced a moment of splendor.

These men were met here at the end of many weeks of work whose strain had left its mark on them. Since the prone body of White Lance had been borne with funereal solemnity from the ship to No. 1 Test Shop, several thousand operations had been performed on it; routine drills, tests, rectification and verification checks had been made and made again until the pace and the stress of concentration had found out weakness in the men while all the time the missile grew stronger in their hands. And there was not one of those several thousand operations that Jim Chapel did not intimately know; there was not one of these men in here—key men, all of them—whom Jim Chapel had not diligently led through a maze of problems and great travail to this moment.

Some had long ago lost their faith in him; his every insistence on a narrower margin of error had made him a new enemy; his disjointed address to the personnel in the hangar had further made them doubt his equilibrium. They had worked on, committed to the project as an end in itself, and had let him lead them, since he was their leader.

Phil Whymlett looked at the slight untidy figure standing in the center of the room and knew that for Jim it was different. He had lost faith in no man, in no part of his own design, in no aspect of the White Lance project, be it technical, scientific, or moral. He could, through these narrow prisms, see the bright erect shape of his missile towering above the deserted terrain. It was all he needed to see. It was all he had been able to see. His vision had shone through the dark of every problem and every doubt, as steady as a beam of light.

The final-warning Klaxon had begun sounding when the G.S.O. had reached the Control Center, and now it died away.

A man asked the principal officer: "Can we go?"

It was now that Phil Whymlett experienced his moment of splendor. It was the feeling one had on watching the flight of an eagle, the stride of a thoroughbred horse, the breasting of a fine ship against a wave. One knew that one watched excellence.

Jim Chapel was looking at nobody; hands in his jacket pockets, his head held sideways in thought, he heard the man's question and did not even look at him nor even speak, but simply nodded. And Whymlett saw in that brief gesture the expression of Jim's unshakable faith in himself, in those who served him, and in White Lance.

The man, turning away, moved the igniter switch.

"No. 1 fuse burning."

Three red lamps came on.

"Pumps holding at full."

"Auxiliary fuse triggered."

"Feed-paths converging. Phase 2."

The red lamps went dark. A green lamp began winking at one-second intervals. "No. 1 fuse active."

"Cut auxiliary."

"Yes, sir."

A batch of lamps glowed green above the S.F.C. panel and the trials control officer began the countdown as a full-dress rehearsal for the shoot.

"Relays active."

Whymlett thought: In ten days or so we'll all be here again, and if Jim is with us we shall have nothing to fear.

"Igniter active."

"Stand-by all circuits."

Through the observation prisms could be seen a wisp of white vapor curling from the bypass valve at the base of the missile.

"Flame-up."

A plume of burnt gas and steam swelled down from the main venturi tubes.

"Missile firing."

The plume billowed and spread to a cloud enveloping the gantry substructure and the first roaring was heard against the walls of the Control Center.

The flight safety officer stood watching his gauges, his hand within an inch of the motor cut-out switch. WL-1 was being static-fired in test conditions and would not leave the launcher, but as F.S.O. he was responsible for cutting the motor in emergency whether flight took place or not.

The roar increased. The scene through the observation prisms was breaking up as exhaust clouds escaped the cooling chute and drifted across the area, hazing the sunlight and sometimes drifting as far as the Control Center, blanking out all vision, then shifting clear and revealing the great shape of the missile.

White Lance came under the full power of the first-stage motor. The progressive discharge of eleven thousand gallons of HTP/Zenox was producing a peak thrust of twenty-eight thousand pounds per square inch at the exhaust tubes, and the force was held by the gantry locks, wind-brace arms, and release jacks. It was the precise force which, in ten days' time, would drive a dead weight of fourteen tons vertically through the atmosphere at eight thousand miles an hour.

The static-firing test was an explosion under control. There was no other way of simulating full-thrust conditions to determine whether or not the fuel was precisely suited to these motors and the motors suited to this vehicle. There was no other way of confirming the hundredfold earlier tests whose findings had been that with this degree of raw force released at the gantry the missile would not break up, the tanks would not burst, the decomposition of critically unstable fuel in massive quantities would not run wild and flood half the island with a tidal wave of flame and bring down every building that was not blast-proof. This was the only way.

Outside vision was now lost totally; the white gas pressed at the windows. Speech was difficult against the monstrous roaring of White Lance; men pitched their voices sharply. Dr. Chapel had moved to watch the main indicator panel and Whymlett was beside him. Everyone had started to sweat, their nerves suffering the bombardment of sound and the stress of concentration and the knowledge that something, somewhere, might go wrong, and that the hand of the F.S.O. might move too late.

The concrete trembled under their feet. Their faces were pale in the fluorescent light and the white glow from the prisms. Whymlett, who had never been in at a major trial, came, over the long seconds, to realize how powerful was the influence of the primitive animal in modern man. He was a scientist, expressing his creative force in terms of intellect. His brain at this moment assured him, by reference to the indicator panels, that an experiment was being conducted under a most elegant system of control and that the risk of cataclysm was minimal. It was the primitive animal in him that warned him, by reference to the senses, that here already was the evidence of cataclysm: the white cloud, spreading a thousand yards from the source of the explosion, pressed at the windows to blind him; the rage of sound encompassed him and made him deaf; the earth itself trembled beneath his feet.

So that a thought was in his head: *We should stop this. We should stop this while we are still safe.*

He was ashamed and had to reason with himself, but the thought remained, until he was forced to look at Jim Chapel beside him, at Jim Chapel's face. Its expression was sublime, serene. This man, who had shown the effects of the stress that had built up in him through these harrowing weeks, even to the point where many doubted him and his ability to go on, was at this moment wholly in possession of himself, and of the missile that thundered out there with the full force of its being.

Whymlett surrendered his fear and the thought went from his mind. Jim was here.

"Pressure dropping. Ninety—"

"Slow pumps—"

"Eighty—"

"Isolate main circuit."

"Reserve chamber coming in—"

"Seventy—"

"Stop primaries—"

"Sixty—"

"Cut off burners."

"Feed-back inactive now."

"Fifty. Fifty, sir."

"All right, let her die."

The roaring was over. Sunlight gilded the frame of the prisms and blue sky showed. Through the thinning glass clouds the missile reappeared, immense and glittering.

Someone hit another switch and a red lamp went dark. The built-in cinecamera was humming, recording the dials as their needles moved.

A man wiped his face. The G.S.O. pushed a button; in a few seconds the roof siren put up a long steady wail, sounding the all clear.

Dr. Chapel gave a nod.

"Thank you, gentlemen."

Chapter 19

On the dying away of the siren all the island was quiet. Among the hundreds of people gathered east of the safety line were some who had been in the London blitz, and they were reminded of it. The thundering had stopped; the all clear had sounded; and they stayed where they were for a minute because there was no hurry now; they were still alive and had all the time in the world.

Colonel Pyne had withdrawn his unit behind a ridge of earth and from there they had watched White Lance. Their view was better than from the Control Center; the exhaust clouds did not reach this far. They saw the missile in true proportion, its bright length standing higher than anything on the island, the gantry-top leaning in the sky. For three and a quarter minutes White Lance was run at full power, its strength sounding across the island and across the ocean; thus had the bull of Minos roared beneath the earth and set men trembling.

The white gas billowed, eddying about the gantry, and at one moment it looked as if the missile had shifted under the strain and was breaking loose, and a man cried out. It was the shadow of the gantry against the drifting cloud; it was the cloud that moved.

Now the siren had gone and there was quiet. The soldiers came away from the ridge of earth.

"By Christ, you can't say they don't know what they're doing over there."

"Twenty-eight thousand at the ducts . . . One of the civvies told me. Twenty-eight . . ."

They were elated.

"All I hope is we'll be here to see her go up."

"I'd give a week's leave for that."

They were proud, now, to be here where great things were done. They trod the earth where White Lance had reared and bellowed, and their ears still rang with the glory of it.

A man laughed for joy. "Twenty-eight thousand . . . Bloody *hell* . . ."

Down by the civilian living quarters people were still talking in groups. Soon they broke up, and the first of them crossed the safety line on their way back to work. Small cars, trucks, and bicycles began filling the transit road, and people begged lifts. A man pedaled slowly down the airstrip, back to his bulldozer that had been acting up on him and wouldn't start. It didn't seem so important now.

Alec Griggs walked back to his office; he had resented the interruption to his work but now he was happy; it had been worth it. The sight and the sound of WL-1 coming through her Phase 5 trial would put new heart into everyone; this shot in the arm had been needed.

A dog ran between the huts, unnerved and whimpering. Someone called to it but it went on running. It would take time to forget a sound as big as that.

Eve Chapel left the group of women she had been with and made her way to the Welfare quarters; before she reached it the security officer's car pulled up alongside, and she stopped. "Can you spare a moment, Mrs. Chapel?" She looked at Hurst. He was holding the door open for her on the other side, and she took exception to his attitude. "I'm really pushed for time, Mr. Hurst. Is it important?" He still held the door. "I think so. We can talk better along the road where there's no one about. It's top secret, you see." His bright smile chilled her and she didn't move.

"Top secrets are not for me, I'm afraid. I've nothing to do with Security."

His smile remained. He looked very cocky today. "But you've very much to do with your own security, haven't you, Mrs. Chapel?"

Coldness came over her.

"I don't know what you mean."

"That's why you ought to get in. Then I can tell you."

She held his stare for as long has she could and then had to look down. A minute ago, she thought, everything had been all right. And now it wasn't. And nothing could ever be all right again.

She walked round the car and got in.

The sun had been up an hour and already the air was warm. The men were coming back from breakfast at the canteen, their voices sounding perkily among the huts.

Colonel Pyne was freshly shaved and spruce-looking, but he had not, thought Sergeant Lacey, slept too well.

"Your phone's just rung, sir, but the caller hung up when I answered. Either that or there's a fault. It happened last evening."

"Why didn't you tell me?"

"I didn't think it was important, sir, the first time."

"It probably isn't."

"Shall I report a fault, sir?"

"No. Just tell me if it happens again."

He went in from the doorway. The bottle was on the bamboo table, still more than half full; he had done better last night, but it had cost him sleep; he would have to learn how to sleep without it; the bottle wasn't the answer.

He listened to the voices of the men; it was a new morning and he was glad for them and envied them.

He had resolved not to go there again, but now he must. That was no fault on the line.

The fuel gauge in the Land-Rover was down to low but he decided to risk it. They could always send out a jerrican. In the driving mirror he saw the wake of the sand dust whirling behind, marking his trail. It didn't matter; he had officially established the habit of touring the island most mornings by the perimeter track. Once beyond the outcrop at the eastern end, even a dust wake couldn't be seen from the camp.

His swimming trunks fluttered and swung from one of the width indicators; he left them there permanently, to dry after his morning swim. It was part of the established habit and he was pleased that they had become known among the men as the "Ken's Own Marine Corps Flag."

After two miles the outcrop gave way to flatter land and the north shore opened out ahead; in another mile he reached the dip where the car would be left hidden from the track and took his swimming trunks, leaving his cap on the seat.

Brilliant light struck from the sea as he climbed down through the rock fissure and came to the roughly made steps. The cove was filled with light and even the dry sand glistened.

She saw him and came toward him, and even before she spoke he knew something was wrong; her face was hunted-looking.

He asked at once: "What's happened?"

"He knows," she said.

It had begun a day or two after the warhead was flown in and stowed in the blockhouse. Pyne had for the first time driven round the island along the deserted perimeter track, stopping the car and just sitting slack at the wheel, needing to be alone, to think, to find a way of accepting what had happened to him and to his company.

He had been given a responsibility he had never expected. Six years in command of a short-range tactical missile unit and growing old . . . Past, surely, the age when they would do this to him. But he had miscalculated; it was experience and stability they looked for, as they did when they picked astronauts—middle-aged men with families, who wouldn't panic when it came to the push. So he was now in charge of a body of men who would, if ordered, unquestioningly destroy a city they had never seen, the ancient seat of emperors, a treasure house of archaeological beauty, the home of five million people who had never heard of him nor would ever know the name of their assassin.

It would have been easier if he had been able to tell Robert and the others.

Sitting at the wheel he had thought of them; already he missed their company and felt estranged; ordinarily he would have joined them for the early dip on the beach not far from the camp.

Someone was coming along the track on a bicycle and he started the engine; it would look odd to be sitting here alone. The Land-Rover was already on the move when he saw who it was and felt obliged to stop. They had not met since the night of the dismal dinner party, though they had acknowledged each other sometimes in the senior mess, from a distance. He felt he had exposed himself more than he had meant—more, perhaps, than she would have wished—at that first meeting, so he had made no attempt to talk to her again. For her own reasons she had seemed content to smile to him across the room and leave it at that.

Now a meeting was unavoidable. She stopped beside the car, straddling her bicycle; he stayed behind the wheel: the engine was still running and it was an excuse not to get out.

"Have you been swimming, Colonel Pyne?"

She had noticed the Ken's Own Marine Corps Flag.

"No. Just carriage exercise."

She looked very young in her overalls; her eyes were clear and her smile was fresh; sea water had dried on her arms, leaving a powdering of white. It was suddenly good to be looking at a young woman with the blue sky behind her; his thoughts had been full of terrible things, the commentaries and photographs that had taken up most of the news space at the time of Hiroshima.

"I swim here every morning," she said, snapping the brake levers up and down, watching him candidly. "There's a beach I've found. No one else knows about it. Only you, now." She smiled quickly, kicking the pedals round and shifting back onto the saddle.

"I won't tell anyone," he said.

"I know."

He watched her in the driving mirror; the sand dust made a haze and the bicycle was soon blotted out.

She said odd things, or the things she said had odd meanings. He thought about her all the way round the island, and it was better than thinking about the other thing.

They had gone down to the cove together three days later. On the days between he had just kept up speed and waved as they passed and she had waved back. Now he pulled up when he saw her, and got out, and they talked for a few minutes about nothing—the water, the heat of the morning even so early, the starkness of the island here where no buildings could be seen.

She had only wanted to show him the cove she had found and the steps she had made in the low cliff, but the water was glass-clear and he changed into his trunks out of sight and swam down the inlet, turning on his back and floating, looking up at her while she laughed in pleasure at seeing him there at his ease in the cool clear water.

They had swum together on the fifth day and he had surface-dived, swimming beneath her and coming up where she didn't expect it, surprising her. They played in the sea like children, and then the innocence went out of it one morning as she lay on her back on the sand, looking up at him with her eyes narrowed against the light. Only then did he realize that it was bound to happen and that he had known it and had done nothing to stop it.

The next day he had run the car into the dip of land to make sure that no one would see it if they passed along the track. From that day onward they had not even acknowledged each other in the senior mess, because it might now be dangerous.

She had made the shell bracelet herself, long before she had known him, selecting the shells carefully for their color, shape, and size; the holes had been difficult, even with the leather tool she borrowed from the Welfare Center; she broke two shells out of three. When she had strung forty or so of them she made a clasp from nylon thread and two small dressmaker's hooks.

The bracelet was a token of the private paradise she had made of the cove, and she wore it most of the time. Ken had admired it, on the third day, and soon afterward on a morning when there was a mist on the early sea and they made love for the first time the bracelet got broken, and she didn't know it until they were leaving and she suddenly saw the shells scattered across the sand.

So it was no longer Paradise.

"We must collect them," he said, "and make a new string." He started down the sand again.

"No. Leave them."

He turned and looked at her, hearing something final in her voice. "But they were beautiful, Eve."

"Yes." She climbed the steps ahead of him and made haste

to find her bicycle; she was gone before he reached the top of the little cliff.

They met again the next day but she didn't mention the bracelet; it belonged to the old world, a little museum piece; already the night tide had flowed over the past and buried the shells in the sand.

"Are you interested in me, Ken?" she asked not many days later.

He smiled, not knowing how to answer. She was curled naked against him in the warmth of the sun.

"Making love," she said, "doesn't presuppose interest." It was pat from the book; there was a chapter about the temptations suffered by husbands when their business took them to strange towns and they were "prey to solicitous women." Such persons, it said, aroused no true interest in a man, even if he fell to their charms.

"I think about you all the time," he said, stroking her short hair, caressing her ear. "Is that a definition of interest?"

He wanted to make light of it but she was serious.

"No one has been interested in me before. I'm not being unkind about Jim. I don't know what he would do—what he'd feel—if I left him or died. I think he loves me but I know I don't interest him, which isn't as funny as it sounds. I am simply there, in his house, like a bathrobe, his favorite and well-loved bathrobe."

He did not interrupt. This had to be said; she had to justify what she was doing, without sounding disloyal.

"I fell in love with a brilliant mind, and with kindness; it was like being near a star that gave off warmth. The dreadful thing is that he's still brilliant and still kind—he hasn't changed, he's still what I fell in love with and that's why I'm so damnably unjust." She held his hard lean body and pressed her face against him, shivering. "I didn't know he wouldn't need me as you do, even if it's for these few hours, and only for this. Oh, God . . . how I need it my-self! Do you think of me as a whore? I don't care—"

He put his fingers against her lips but she jerked her head away—"Men need whores and if they didn't there wouldn't be any—"

"Listen," he said, drawing her face against him as if she were a child, "a whore is a woman who doesn't do it for love."

"Love? You mean who doesn't love it, love doing it." Her hands dug into his arm. "Then I'm no whore . . . it's all I live for, now."

After that day she never spoke about her marriage, nor of anything that did not spring to her tongue from the heat of their lovemaking. As with the famished, her hunger, once aroused, was unassuageable.

Later she saw by chance one of her shells, with a hole in it, exposed by the running of the tides, and remembered the virginal care with which she had made the bracelet; wryly she thought of it now as her maidenhead.

Some time before the static trial of White Lance was made, she waited almost an hour for Ken and he didn't come, and the next morning he gave no real explanation. She tried to make him promise always to come, but he made no promise. He was difficult to talk to—or he found it difficult to talk, but she sensed he was tiring of her, or of her fierce physical demands, and regretted urging him to promise.

"Every other day, then," she told him. "Please come every other day."

"It's not that I don't want to, Eve." He would have liked to tell her the simple truth: this couldn't last; it was a fever, not love; and it would be easier to let it die away than to finish abruptly with each other. He couldn't put that into words. There was more: he had been on a spiritual holiday; instead of taxing himself with thoughts of his responsibilities he had lain with a girl on the shores of each new day, as naked as it had been in Eden and as far from the known world; he had come to understand her when she said that if they climbed the cliff steps and saw that the radio mast and control tower had vanished it would be no surprise. But gradually his thoughts came back to the realities: the concrete blockhouse and his constant fear of receiving a signal that would thrust him face to face with the need to decide, one way or the other. The city of Peking was not a mirage; it lay in Latitude 40, Longitude 112, range 3750, elevation 76.

Should a man whose hands held life or death for five million people be found rutting like an animal each time the sun rose? Dear God, he must be out of his mind . . .

The holiday was over, but he compromised and went to the cove every other day, despising himself for his weakness. The rot was setting in. The inexcusable scene in the senior mess, the faces of his own officers shocked by his lack of control . . . The blatant disobedience of orders in telling Robert a thing he should have held most secret . . . He would have better told him: I'm having an affair with the wife of the principal officer—say what you think of me and don't spare your words, it's the only way you can help me . . .

He had shrunk even from the idea of putting such a thing into words. He wanted help from no one; he must help himself. There were two decisions to be made, and for the first time in his life he found himself incapable of making them, and wondered how it was that so gross a weakness in a man could show itself so late.

He must break off the affair with Eve, or he must choose to let it go on indefinitely. He must prepare himself to obey any signal that was received from London, or he must resign his commission before a signal could commit him to the unthinkable.

174

On the morning when Sergeant Lacey reported to him about the telephone, and he drove to the north shore and saw Eve waiting for him with anguish in her face, he knew that he was too late and that these decisions were no longer his to make.

Chapter 20

Looking up at his face she realized he was a stranger. The amber eyes and the long mouth, the way he tilted his head when she amused him, the straight back and the iron hardness of his limbs, the firmness of his hands—all these things she knew intimately and they were no part of the strangeness; still, he was a stranger, because whatever they had done it had not touched the heart.

"Who?" he asked her. "Who knows?"

"Hurst."

His eyes widened, then he gave a short laugh in his throat—"*Hurst* . . ."

She moved away, treading carefully on the sand as if rough movement would break something; and in a moment he followed her and took her gently by the shoulder.

"Are you sure, Eve?"

"Yes."

"Tell me what happened."

"He took me in his car where we couldn't be overheard. He's been—watching us for a long time. For weeks." She had difficulty in saying it; her mouth seemed bruised by every word. "He has field glasses. Long before we—before we met here, he used to watch me swimming." Very slowly she whispered from a white face, "I think he is the most disgusting man I have ever known."

He said as softly, "I may kill him." She was shocked at the savagery in his voice.

"No, Ken. Nothing stupid. It's too serious for that."

"Not in cold blood, but I'll have to talk to him and it may come to it." The bottle had smashed against the wall, surprising him: he hadn't known he would do it. "Why did he tell you this?"

"I don't know." She tried to speak normally, to calm him. He was a person of great reserve and he valued privacy, and now he knew they had been watched in the most private act of all. Murder had been done for less than that. "I think it was just to gloat," she said.

"What did he want? What did he demand?"

"Nothing—"

"*Nothing?* We are in his hands and he asks for nothing?"

An idea was in his mind: to come here tomorrow, as they so often had, in the hope that Hurst would follow them again. Let her show herself, swimming, while he tracked the man's vantage point—it couldn't be far. In cold blood, then, better still.

"He just wants to feel he has power over us," she said.

"And not use it?"

"*The civilian will be escorted to the boundary. Any resistance will be met by force.*"

And Hurst had said: "*Enjoy yourself. You won't be here very long.*"

The surf touched their feet.

She said: "I don't know what to do." It was not addressed to him; she was staring at the sea, perhaps speaking to it as a sailor speaks when he is lost and the sky is blackening. "I don't know what to do."

"There's nothing you need do. Leave him to me. He's mine."

His eyes frightened her. "There are two of us, Ken.

We'll think of something between us. We can persuade him, in some way—"

"*Persuade?*" He, too, spoke with his face to the sea. It was their world; they had lived with the sea every morning as the sun came higher; they had not been able to see, from here, the radio mast and the control tower.

A man of Hurst's kind wouldn't be open to persuasion. He'd have his terms and if they weren't met he would let hell loose for the pleasure of it: a word to Chapel at this stage of the White Lance shoot . . . a word to the War Office . . .

"Was it worth it, Ken?" She stood shivering and spoke almost lightly, looking up at him. "He wants you thrown out of Tokariji, we might as well talk about it. You made him lose face that time in the weapon pit—Robert told me."

"If those are his terms I can meet them; my time's up, here. But there's you, Eve. If—"

"Don't worry. I'll ask for time, persuade him to keep his peace until after the White Lance shoot; then I'll tell Jim myself—I'd sooner he heard it from me than anyone else." Her calmness worried him. "We've got to cut loose, Ken, that's all, in our different ways."

She took his hand suddenly and they walked toward the cliff where she had made the steps, passing the smooth rock where she used to lie on her front and dry herself in the sun, alone and feverish and dreaming of the male of her species. She would not be here again; no sign that she had ever been here would be left, except, sometimes when the tide disturbed the sand, a few shells prettier than the rest.

Standing on the perimeter road, with the radio mast cutting the sky, it was easier to think straight and she said: "Please don't do anything that would make it worse for us all. It's a case for parleying, not war."

"He may try to talk to you again. If he does, refer him to me. I'm asking you to do that."

"I can't promise, Ken. I think I'm better at parleying than you, and most of the fright's gone, now, because we've talked about it and you've given me strength. Some time later it'll hit me and I'll have to face what it's cost you. It's just that we didn't think of the risk. That's nothing new."

It was man's most powerful urge, the book said, and in circumstances where yielding would lead to folly and the hurt of others it must be ruthlessly sublimated by healthy activities such as tennis, hiking, or Swedish dancing, and the mind occupied in welfare work, charity organization, or efficient home management.

Why Swedish dancing? It seemed an odd thing to throw in.

Ken was standing very still in the grip of thought, his eyes narrowed and his mouth in a hard line. She touched his hand and smiled.

"Cheer-o, then."

For the first time his heart was reached, and he knew it would be less easy now to forget her.

"Do this for me," he said with slow urgency. "Don't go near that man, even to "parley," as you call it. I shall be seeing him myself, some time today, and if he gives me reason to think that he'll go to your husband I shall make quite sure that he doesn't."

She wouldn't have believed that rage could be expressed in a tone so low, in words so ordinary. She had seen this unblinking gaze in cats when they stole upon a bird.

There was nothing she could say; he would do what he must and she couldn't stop him, so she turned away and walked quickly to the rock where she had left her bicycle, her hands dug into the pockets of her overalls and bunched up hard as the fright began coming back.

The chief security officer was writing at his desk. The air conditioner rushed softly, full on, but the thermometer on the wall still showed ninety-three degrees. The sunblinds were lowered across the south windows but the east window was unobstructed so that traffic could be seen along the road from the living quarters.

When he saw the army car pull up outside he stopped writing for a moment and considered with pleasure what was about to happen. Colonel Pyne, D.S.O., M.C., was going to eat humble pie.

The whole operation had gone well. Quite a few months ago he had noticed Mrs. Chapel riding her bicycle most mornings along the perimeter track eastward, and he had become interested because there were no buildings in that direction, nowhere to go, no one to call on. So he had followed her at a safe distance; he liked to know what people were doing; it was his job. Security was most affected when emotions were aroused, and when people did odd things it was usually emotional at source. Sexuality, especially homosexuality, was often a prime mover in cases of security breach; you could think of a dozen names that had been in the headlines in the last couple of years alone. There was probably nothing sexual about a bicycle ride but Mrs. Chapel had formed an odd habit and he wanted the first piece of a possible new jigsaw puzzle.

It was at first disappointing; she had merely taken to the idea of a solitary morning swim. Then there was a little excitement; he hadn't seen many women naked before and although he had to park his car some distance from the cove the field glasses were powerful. It made a pleasant morning exercise for him whenever pressure of work allowed him the time. It was agreeable in the evenings as well, when he saw her in the senior mess. How many of the men there had seen her as he had? It was a comfortable feeling of power over them.

There wasn't much of a jigsaw here, just the one piece. After a while he stopped following her, because you could get bored with watching the same thing too often. But he watched her with more interest when he saw her about the place and sometimes made occasion to speak to her in the senior mess, at one time complimenting her on her dress, which was of course a joke she couldn't share.

Then he was on to it—the second piece of the jigsaw. It was a few weeks ago, when Colonel Pyne had come into the mess. Normally when he and Mrs. Chapel saw each other they smiled and sometimes exchanged a word; this time they didn't even acknowledge each other.

You had to watch for little things like that.

He began watching Pyne. Three days later he had them together in the field glasses. Observation was made half a dozen times; it was rather embarrassing; they looked like thin pigs, with no clothes on.

Of course there was no evidence, only his word, and if he went straight to Pyne the fellow might simply deny it—a man like him could keep up a solid front when he wanted. He would also warn Mrs. Chapel that they'd been seen, and tell her to deny it as well. Between them they could get away with it, because they'd be sure to behave themselves in future. There'd be no proof. Proof was everything.

So he had gone to the lady first and although she didn't admit anything—didn't say a word—she was obviously upset; by her attitude she thought it was a fair cop, with no hope of any denials. And the way was clear: she'd go straight to Pyne and he'd see it was too late to do anything. And Pyne would come to him, to try blustering it out. It was most important for him to come here, to this office.

The army car was standing outside.

He began writing again and didn't look up when the door opened. Sunlight flashed across the room and then the door slammed shut.

"Whoever you are," he said, going on writing, "you might care to knock, next time. This is the security office."

The man's shadow darkened half the desk.

"What are your terms?"

Hurst was pleased to hear the anger in the tone; it was the anger of fright. He used the blotting paper and placed it neatly beside the report book before looking up into Pyne's face. The man was hardly recognizable; he looked quite ill.

"Good morning." He never used a name or a title with people, except for the principal officer, a man to be respected. The others were all the same to him—boffins, visiting Foreign Office men, army types—they interested him in one thing only: they were a security risk or they weren't. "What can I do for you?"

"I've come to know your terms." The voice still shook a little but the man seemed to be getting himself under control.

"Won't you sit down? Then you can tell me what you're talking about." He got up and went to the big steel filing cabinet, pushing the doors shut.

"Come on, Hurst, you've got certain information about me and I want to hear your terms for keeping it to yourself."

Hurst came back to his desk but didn't sit down.

"You mean your little game with the principal officer's wife?"

Pyne was having to take a visible grip on himself, straightening his back till you could swear there was a broomstick under his shirt. "It concerns Mrs. Chapel, yes."

"M'm . . . And what makes you think I'd pass on the news?"

"I'm a judge of men. In going out of your way to spy on the private lives of others you exhibit the morals of a guttersnipe, and in speaking first to the lady instead of to me you show yourself to be a filthy little coward—or worse, the type of pervert who derives satisfaction in holding power over women. You are therefore more than capable of embarrassing me by spreading any dirt you imagine to exist, and—"

"Now just a minute, will you?" He could feel his neck reddening. He didn't like being called names, especially by this fellow. "You'd better be more careful, don't you think? If you want to talk about morals, I've quite a few ideas on that subject myself. And you're in a tricky position, you know. If I choose to, I can have you thrown out of Tokariji —tomorrow."

"You can." Very clipped, proper army-style.

"And I can finish you off. Career, reputation, all chance of a decent future. Wipe you up. Okay?"

"Yes, you can do all that to me."

"Well, I'm glad you admit it. The point is, you can't come in here calling me names." The man really did have a nerve. "Now let's talk respectably, shall we? You ask me to give you my 'terms.' What terms? There aren't any, you see. You can't stop me from doing whatever I think fit, can you? What can you offer, to save your neck? Nothing. So it's no good talking about 'terms.'"

The air conditioner rushed softly. Pyne had an odd look. The control kept slipping, then he got it back; it was like someone constantly hitching up his trousers.

"Then tell me your intentions."

"Ah. I can see you're worried about that. You think I intend getting you thrown out of here and court-martialed?"

"I do."

"Why should I?"

"Because you are the type to take easy revenge."

Hurst picked up his pen from the desk and toyed with it, unscrewing the cap and screwing it the wrong way; the threads made little clicks.

"I'm going to overlook your insolence," he said slowly and with enjoyment. "As I've told you before, once a certain sort of man gets a pip on his shoulder he goes trotting about trying to boss everyone, civilians included. But we'll skip that. The thing is, you're not such a good judge of men, you see. What do I want 'revenge' for? You overrode my authority the other day and had me marched off the premises, which was embarrassing for me as a security officer; but I don't break a man and his career just for playing the martinet. Good heavens, if I wanted to break people I wouldn't know where to start! In my job I get hold of a lot of information, especially in a small place like Tokariji—you'd be quite surprised. No, all I want is for a wrong to be righted. I'll tell you what my intentions are. You'll order your men on parade in a day or so, when I've got the time to be present, and you'll make a personal apology to me in front of them."

He gave one of his quick disarming smiles. Pyne didn't seem to appreciate it. He answered with one very odd word.

"No."

His eyes had narrowed and he was breathing hard. He had the look of men Hurst had seen in the tropics, when they were going "troppo"—off their heads.

"No? You mean you refuse to make a simple apology?"

"I do. I consider I was perfectly in my rights to order—" he had some difficulty in getting it out, perhaps because he wanted to sound dignified "—to order a civilian off army bounds, and I consider there is no proper case for an apology."

Hurst began losing patience with the man.

"You'd rather I had you thrown out of here, then?"

"If you choose to do it."

"Rather than make an apology?"

"Certainly."

Pyne was really off his head. He must be as ill as he looked.

"Well I do think there's a case for an apology," said Hurst, "and I intend having it. If I don't, then I'll have no choice but to see you're ordered out of here ignominiously —isn't that the proper word for it?"

Pyne said nothing. His shoulders had drooped an inch and he pulled them straight. Hurst couldn't quite see what was in the man's mind. An apology wasn't much to ask for, but he was determined to have it. He could put the top brass onto this soldier and finish off his whole career, but that was going to extremes, and even if the whole of the army unit knew who it was that had wiped the floor with their precious commanding officer it wouldn't be the same. No, this fellow had marched him off in front of all those people, and he would have to apologize in front of them. It was perfectly simple. Pyne was speaking again, very clipped, his eyes still narrowed and his face blotchy. "I refuse your demands, Hurst. I shan't change my mind on that point. There will be no apology. There is one other question. What are you intending to do about Mrs. Chapel?"

This was another surprise. "You'll have to explain yourself."

"Very well. Owing to your habit of prying, you have a certain advantage over her, too obvious to define. Do you intend to use it?"

"I've not thought about that, as yet. I'll have to think about it. But I can't quite see why I should make her suffer for something that you did."

Pyne seemed surprised himself by that. It took him a minute to answer, and when he did it was like one of those people on the stage in a memory act; they just spoke without any feeling, reeling off facts like a dummy with a loud-speaker inside.

"I would be glad to believe you but I must tell you this. You may take whatever action you choose with regard to myself but if you try to harm Mrs. Chapel, if you try to talk to her again and embarrass her, if you go to Dr. Chapel and tell him what you know, if you try to harm either of them in any way because of what I have done, then I will smash you, Hurst, physically smash you up, whatever the consequences."

Hurst saw that a vein was beating in his neck; there were patches of sweat spreading on his shirt; his eyes looked bloodshot under their narrowed lids.

"Well, I wouldn't make any more threats like that. They don't bother me. If I were you I'd go away and calm down a bit and then do some straight thinking. When I want to talk to you again I'll send for you, and you'd better be ready to parade your men and make your apology to me in front of them. That's all."

He'd hardly finished speaking before Pyne turned on his heel and jerked the door open. The sunlight flashed across Hurst's eyes, making him blink.

When he had seen the army car drive off he stood for a minute thinking, trying to fathom out how a man could prefer to throw up his whole career than make a decent apology when he was in the wrong. Surely he'd calm down and come round to it. He'd have to.

The sound of the air conditioner reminded him about the tape and he opened the doors of the big filing cabinet, automatically switching off the recorder. Then he cut the tape and stuck on the tab marked 387, the code number for Colonel Pyne. It was better than just evidence; you could call it a full confession.

Chapter 21

The conference had lasted since early morning and now it was breaking up, not long before noon. A few stayed on for a final word with the P.O. They were the ones who had supported him in the clash of opinions—Follett, Brayworth, Phil Whymlett. The ashtrays were littered; pads and pencils lay strewn on the long table; the blackboard was filled with equations, diagrams, figures and symbols, and the floor beneath was scattered with chalk stubs that had broken in Chapel's emphatic hands.

"Did we win?" he asked the few who had stayed.

Phil Whymlett said: "Some. And some we lost." He wished Jim would sit down again, or go home and sleep and go on sleeping. They could wait.

A lot of modifications had been accepted without argument. Deflector plates would have to be built at the opening of the cooling duct below White Lance to prevent exhaust gas and steam from drifting across the apron: it had blanked off the vision panels in the Control Center during the static-firing test and it would obstruct instrumentation on the day of the shoot. There were other things; a thicker wall for the main pump bypass installation to correct surge due to vibration; Mark VI retros in the feedback system instead of Mark V, to take care of pressure; a new metering jet for the induction, because the present jet had shown oxidization traces under the fluoroscope.

It was when Chapel had come down to margins of tolerance again that the struggle began. Two of the Wymark-Vincent team had just walked out; of those remaining, most had gone after him without pretense of courtesy; the shoot was a matter of days now and it wasn't the time to polish the soles of their shoes, as McLean had called it.

Some of them, seeing the feverish look in Chapel's face, seeing his adamant fingers break chalk after chalk as he tried to drive home his convictions, seeing him sway on his feet more than once, kept silent half hoping he would break down completely and be forced to rest while they ironed out the final snags in peace.

They felt pity for him; no one watching him could feel unmoved; he was a sick man keeping himself going by willpower. But unless he got a grip on himself he was going to wreck the shoot, and they weren't going to let him. The difficulty was that he was the designer of the missile as well as P.O., Tokariji; he wielded too much power, or he wielded more power than he had.

"We'll take it from here," Whymlett told him and felt for a cigarette and found the packet empty and chucked it down. "They'll do the mods we've agreed on, and if there's enough time they'll do the rest."

Chapel turned away. "We shoot when we are ready. Until we are ready there's enough time." His chest was hurting. Some kind of cramp. There wasn't enough air to breath.

"Lunch break," said Follett, trying to sound cheerful. He could no more touch a biscuit than fly. Chapel's look of exhaustion exhausted him; for the first weeks of the preparation sequence he'd been up against the P.O., resenting his encroachment on his domain as missile officer at every turn. Then he had come to see what White Lance was growing into: an instrument of near perfection the like of which he had never known.

When they left the Instrumentation Building, Phil Whymlett asked: "How's Evie today, Jim?"

"I think she's better. She had some breakfast, I think."

Eve had spent yesterday in bed with what she called tummy trouble. She had looked pale and headachy, most unusual for her; it had worried him. He had offered to send a doctor along but she said she just wanted quiet.

The sun hurt his eyes as he crossed the installation area with Phil; he had left his dark glasses somewhere. Mary hadn't been in her office when they had left, or she would have given him some more glasses. What would he do without Mary? What would he do without Eve?

Eve shouldn't be ill, it worried him.

Going into the mess he looked to his left as he always did; he tried not to look but it was instinctive. The long finger of the Triton pointed at the sky; he would like to smash it, blow it up; it pointed to hopelessness.

The next day they went into Phase 7, taking the head component from the test shop to Area 1 and hoisting it to the gantry. Whymlett watched the operation like a cat with kittens; everything he had done in the last two years was packed into this component: a history of unremitting labor and sleepless nights, of insoluble problems that were finally solved, even of his private life (his wife had been hospitalized with appendicitis the night when a transverse layout had burnt up and set them back six months), was now recorded in a pattern of electronic systems only a little less complex than a human brain, and it now became the head of White Lance.

Phase 7 was the last; it was the shoot phase. The realization haunted everyone as they went through the last few thousand manipulations, working high up in the gantry, higher than steeplejacks. The solid-fuel cuckoo motor had gone in; it had to go in with the head component; thus there were safety officers, fire-control teams, and medical staffs in attendance on the ground and in the gantry itself.

It was quiet work and the technicians spoke very seldom. If something was wrong inside the main body or the head component, or if there were a flaw in the solid motor, it was too late to do anything now, and they knew it and did not like it.

Irving, ground safety, watched everything; there wasn't a man who wouldn't swear that the G.S.O. wasn't standing behind him—behind *him*, personally—the whole of the time. Some cursed him; some could still remember he was there to save their lives. The work went on.

In the final operations there were only two incidents and they happened on the same day. Someone dropped a tool and it struck a girder a hundred feet below and bounced off, hitting the ground near one of the ambulances. Everyone stopped work and just did nothing, trying not to think about it. Irving got to the man within half a minute and found him shaking uncontrollably. Without asking him why the tool hadn't been tied to a securing line, without saying anything to him at all, he led him to the gantry lift and took him down, handing him over to a nurse.

The tool—a linkage gauge the size of a small wrench—was made mostly of steel. It would have killed anyone in its path when it landed, not far from where the ambulance crew were standing, but nobody thought about that; they thought about the spark it must have made in bouncing off the girder within a few feet of the solid-fuel motor. No one would have had a chance.

The second incident came at the end of the afternoon. There had been trouble with one of the head component sabot-ring clamps and at first it looked serious because a welding job *in situ* would mean removing the whole cuckoo motor first to comply with safety regulations. A group of specialists gathered at the spot, and the principal officer was with them. So was the G.S.O.

After an hour's work the clamp was reset and tested for alignment. Dr. Chapel alone was not satisfied. It took another hour to fetch special instruments from No. 1 Test Shop, realign and recheck six times. Then they stood in silence, not looking at the P.O. as he made a final check himself with the help of a technician. They knew he was going to say no again. They were wrong.

"Yes. I will pass it."

The sun was six diameters above the western sea and the work would go on for another hour. Irving made sure that nobody heard him speak to Dr. Chapel.

"I think you should go down now and get some sleep."

He had seen Chapel, a minute ago, pass a hand over his face and with the other hand reach out for the nearest support.

"We haven't finished." He stared at the G.S.O. as if he couldn't remember who he was. "The sun is still up." He turned his head slowly and looked out across the gantry rail. "Isn't it?"

"I've got to ask you to go down now, sir, and go to bed. Doc Friedmann will give you something to make you sleep."

With anyone but the principal officer he would simply make it an order and that would be that. A man in this condition was dangerous.

"I'm perfectly well, Irving, don't worry." He made to turn away but Irving said:

"I can't allow you to remain in the gantry. I'd like you to come down with me right away. You'll be right as rain after a good night's sleep." He held the P.O.'s arm. "Don't make it difficult for me, sir."

For an instant he saw Chapel's eyes brighten into some-

thing like anger and he even got two words out in a rush
—"I refuse—"

"You can't, sir." He tightened the hold on his arm. "I'm
your safety officer. These are your men up here, seventy of
them. It's for us to look after them, isn't it?"

Chapel did not move. He saw Irving's face against the
background of buildings below, far below. The ground
looked solid; there was no impression of height; one would
not fall from here; but the linkage gauge had fallen; that
had been terrible; and Eve should not be ill; the Triton
should not be there; unthinkable . . . unthinkable . . .

"—Asleep before you know it—"

"What?"

Irving held his arm. They walked round the gallery to
the elevator. Chapel said vaguely:

"The height. It's just the height."

"Of course. Some people never get used to it. I never do,
myself."

They talked quite normally in the elevator. Chapel spoke
aloud to himself for the most part, going over technical
stuff that was lost on Irving. They took the nearest car
and drove to the living quarters, where Dr. Friedmann had
his consulting room.

Friedmann saw them getting out of the car and knew
what had happened. It had been going to happen for a long
time; it had only been a question of waiting.

Chapel said only one thing to the G.S.O. when they
were inside the cool green-tinted room.

"I will trouble you not to look at me like that." He tried
to stop his hands; they had gone mad in the jacket pockets,
digging, digging—"Have you never seen fatigue in a man
before?"

"Has its known point."

Her face grew large and brightness fell from her eyes.

Her hand had always felt like this on his own; he would know the touch of this hand anywhere.

"Its known point on the earth's surface."

Warmth splashed onto his face.

"My head aches," he said, a flat statement. The thought train was broken and he was annoyed. "Every trajectory-measuring instrument has its known point on the earth's surface. It must. It must."

"Don't talk, Jim."

At the sound of her voice he opened his eyes fully.

"You are crying, Eve."

"No." She went away.

He was annoyed again, tried to sit up, and managed it before she came back. His head throbbed and he remembered Friedmann had given him a damned pill. The after-effects.

"You shouldn't get up, Jim."

"I've got up. What were you talking about the known point for?"

"I don't know," she said.

"What's the time?"

"I'll ring Dr. Friedmann. Please don't get out of bed."

"All right."

He took his chance and was in the bathroom before she returned, cleaning his teeth, his left hand steadying him on the edge of the basin. She didn't knock on the door but he knew she'd be there listening in case he fell over. It was annoying.

But she wasn't there when he came out, and he missed her and called toward the stairs while he was dressing. She came into the room.

"Was it me you were calling?"

"Yes."

"Did you want something?"

"I wanted you."

She went out quickly for some reason and he heard her blowing her nose on the stairs.

Pulling his trousers on he nearly fell over but managed to stop himself with the help of the wardrobe door; the whole thing shook and his box of studs went clattering down.

"Jim!"

"What's the matter?"

She came into the room. "I thought you'd fallen."

"I tripped."

He wished people would not look at him like that. He was only tired.

"Dr. Friedmann says he hopes you'll call in on him."

"I am too busy." He knotted his tie, not very well; it would have to do.

"He only wants you to take an antidote against the after-effects of the sleeping pill."

"I can do with that, certainly."

She entreated him: "Please call there."

"It's on my way." The darkness—his own personal terrifying darkness—was coming on him again and he moved quickly about the room; movement was the only way to keep it back. He knew why he had been talking, now, about the known point; he had wakened with the thought on his mind. He was like a trajectory-measuring instrument; he had a place for his feet on the earth's surface but he had suddenly lost it, the known point.

He found himself standing in front of the window looking at the radio mast. He could see the nose cone of Colonel Pyne's Triton.

"There ought to be a way," he said, "of exorcising evil." He was strangely uncertain whether he was speaking aloud or silently thinking. "When a dog goes mad they shoot it. We always ought to shoot mad dogs." He felt in his pockets and took the comfort from the feel of familiar things: Pencils, miniature slide rule, magnifying lens, keys, penknife.

"Is there anything I can do, Jim?"

She stood near. He felt her near him; the dark could never creep in when she was close by. Did she know? He couldn't tell her, because it would mean telling about the dark, too.

"No. Just be there, somewhere." He turned and looked at her; she had been crying. "You mustn't be miserable, Eve. There's nothing to worry about."

"No."

She didn't smile. That was disturbing, worse than anything else, even crying.

"We're all working up to the shoot," he said. "All feeling the strain a bit."

He wanted to stay with her but there was no time. White Lance had begun more than four years ago and now there was only a few days left. Perhaps she would come to the gantry and watch the final operations. He didn't like to ask her because rockets bored her.

As he left the room she said urgently—"I feel so useless to you."

"The opposite is true. You are the known point now."

She stayed by the window. The radio mast looked no more now than it was.

It was no good ringing Dr. Friedmann; it was his job to reassure her, if necessary by lying. But he must see that nothing happened to Jim. Friedmann, Irving, Phil—he had good men about him.

She was shivering and went into the window bay to stand with her back to the direct sunshine, but the shivering went on. How was it that she was now so fearful for Jim and so aching to protect him and help him, when such a little time ago she had risked hurting him and destroying his peace of mind? She hadn't been certain that no one would see them in the cove by the north shore; she'd risked it.

Jim could still be hurt and his peace of mind still be destroyed. Hurst had only to tell him. Ken had said he had seen Hurst and "arranged things" and that it would be all right: if she went to see him herself it might mess things up. But the risk was there.

Ken was already hurt and most of him was destroyed. Had it been worth it, for him? No. He'd already started keeping away from the cove. There was something in the book about that; they called it the "satiation point" beyond which there was no true pleasure in "the act." What was it like, the feeling of having had so much that you didn't want it any more for a time? She would never know, now.

Ken would be going. She couldn't go with him even if Jim wasn't hurt by it. Ken was a stranger and always would be; she could never live with him. But you don't destroy a man because you can't live with him, and at the same time risk destroying the man with whom you can. Both these things she had done.

The air in the room was still. A mote of dust floated across the patch of sunshine and she envied and hated its indifference when there was so much desperately to be done against the fear that there was in fact nothing, nothing to be done. Warmth filled her throat again and as the salt of the first tear stung her lips she thought of shutting the door, but no one would hear her in an empty house.

The ground safety officer had a word with Friedmann in the lunch break. "What's your opinion?"

"I've had another talk with him this morning." The large eyes brooded in the pale face.

"And?"

"I don't think I can form any real opinion yet."

Irving said quietly: "I think you can."

Friedmann was gazing around. Nobody was near. He asked: "How many days before the shoot?"

"Five, six."

"Then I think all you can do to help everyone is to carry on with the job and spread the impression that he'll be able to hold out that long."

"You don't think he will?"

"No."

Chapter 22

Dr. Friedmann did not regret having given Irving his opinion; he regretted there had been no choice. Of all the establishment personnel the G.S.O. was the man to be told if a rocket motor looked ready to blow up or a major fire broke out. Or the principal officer were heading for a breakdown. He had tried to evade it but Irving had nailed him down; it had been better to tell him suspect; a man like Irving worked best on facts.

Friedmann's worry was that his opinion wasn't conclusive. There could be elements influencing Dr. Chapel's behavior that were good or bad, that would hasten a collapse or protect him from it. There was one element he was sure, but he couldn't name it.

On the face of it Chapel was suffering from overwork on a missile of his own design that had to succeed for the sake of his self-respect and reputation. Below this were the understones that had more meaning: Chapel and the army man, Pyne, were bitterly opposed ideologically. Chapel, fervently pacifist following his trauma at the time of Hiroshima, saw Pyne as the very demon of war.

Question: if Pyne and his missile had not come to Tokariji, would Chapel be in this state now, even overworking as he was? It seemed unlikely.

Deeper still: the Chapels' marriage was not whole. Mrs.

Chapel was sex frustration personified, at least until more recently when she had become more vital and confident in herself. (A liaison? Possibly. But Chapel didn't know, therefore it didn't worry him.) But where was *his* sex being expressed? In White Lance. And he was scared of failure—of another failure, after the BJ-9 flop. Scared of impotence. Nothing must spoil the shoot—the orgasm. *Especially in front of Pyne*, whose erection, though in one way less powerful, was more powerful in that it was an aggressive weapon and designed to make the war that Chapel hated.

Guilt (Hiroshima); fear (of impotence); and sex (with Pyne his rival). You could explain a man's breakdown by references to any one of those influences alone. But there was a missing component and Friedmann still could not put a finger on it. He already thought of it as Influence X; he had spent so much thought on it that he knew everything about it, except what it was.

It was to do with Pyne, or Pyne's missile. It was somewhere in the area. Chapel referred to it obliquely in every conversation. "There ought to be a way," he had said this morning, "of cutting out evil, physically, with a knife, as we do cancer." He had been standing at this window, looking across the tamarisk hedge toward the army camp, when he had said it.

Mrs. Chapel was no help. She came to see him soon after Chapel left. All she could do was to confirm that the presence of the army unit worried her husband. On her own relations with him she was less certain, and Friedmann gave her the simplest advice on the grounds that if it did no good it could do no harm:

"He misses seeing you around. However decorative you are in his house, however attentive, he doesn't see you in the context of his work—and outside the context of his work he can hardly see *anything*. Dreary but true. Most of them are like that, these rarified intelligences. Terrific focus but no accommodation. Why don't you go and make tea for them or something?"

"I'd be in the way."

"You don't actually have to crawl in and out of the rocket."

Her smile didn't come easily; he believed she'd been crying; her eyes looked a little pink. That was to the good; the more upset she was by Chapel's condition the better she could help.

"I've always kept off his preserves," she said.

He hitched himself onto the edge of his desk and said: "Or put it another way, you've always shown disinterest in what most absorbs him. That's how he might see it."

"I don't think so. And how would I begin? It'd be like the charwoman holding the telescope for the Astronomer Royal —he'd just wish I'd go!" She moved about restlessly. "How can I commune with a brain like his—when it's actively working? Other people feel like this, you know; we've talked about it. His own secretary—you know Mary White—she can only just about stand it, and she works in the Instrumentation Building . . ."

In all those years, Friedmann thought, the P.O.'s wife hadn't got around to a working relationship.

"He's not solely a brain, Mrs. Chapel. Nobody is. He's got a heart. And he needs you."

She looked away. "Yes, I know, but it's not enough. People need a drink, they need some money. It's not enough to be a—a bottle of Coca-Cola or a sixpenny bit."

"No, it's not. But he's parched with thirst and flat broke and could use the magnum of champagne and the crock of gold that you represent."

He had never seen much of the Chapels since he'd come to Tokariji; in these few minutes his eyes were being opened. It was a commonplace that the sons of famous men were often cramped by the paternal eminence; it could happen also to their wives.

He said: "I'm going to talk personally, Mrs. Chapel. I don't know if you're aware of your reputation among the personnel—we seldom know what people think about us. But you're regarded as a perfect partner for the principal officer: charming, unobtrusive, a faultless hostess, and an invaluable influence in the establishment, tackling a score of jobs from entertaining distinguished visitors to helping in the laundry and the Welfare Section. In the last few minutes you've compared yourself to a charwoman, a bottle of Coca-Cola, and a sixpenny bit. That kind of self-belittlement doesn't help anybody in any relationship, least of all in a marriage."

He smiled hesitantly. "We began by talking about Dr. Chapel and we finished by talking about you, and it may well be the way in—to help him."

She didn't say anything, but she seemed to have been listening and to be thinking about it. He knew how much he had left unsaid: it concerned her need of her husband, and its nature. That could be talked over some other time and he would leave her with a hint.

"There may be a lot of other things that want bringing into the light, but time is getting close; not long, and we shoot. The vital thing for the moment, Mrs. Chapel, is that however you want to regard yourself, champagne or Coca-Cola, the need is his, not yours, and I know that you can fulfill it, and will want to. A cup of tea up on the gantry there might be a start."

When the principal officer's car drew up at the base of the gantry a group of key personnel were there waiting for him; the news that he was back at work after an enforced rest had just been telephoned to them in Area 1. They had questions for him that couldn't wait.

"The 24-channel Webster doesn't tie in with the secondary system, Dr. Chapel. Weight margin's five kilos."

"Use the 28-channel."

"When does the 'Covery optics team go out?"

"Now. They should have gone already."

"There's condensation inside the bell-housing on 290-A, sir. We wipe and plug up, or use open heat?"

"Use heat, but warn the G.S.O. you're doing it."

"The slaving beam has just been checked. Will you be checking yourself?"

"Of course."

They followed him across the apron, breaking off as he answered their questions until only one man was left, and all he asked was: "How're you feeling, Jim?"

It was Phil Whymlett. Chapel said: "I feel very good. Why not?" They got into the gantry elevator together.

On this day—Day 2, Phase 7—eighty per cent of the personnel was fully engaged; the remainder had finished work in the tests shops and early-sequence sections and they would have nothing more to do; White Lance had passed into a phase beyond their involvement. Of the people now engaged, half were in Area 1 and the rest were manning the instrumentation. These operators had nothing to do with the missile itself but would be tracking it in four days' time during the shoot, and final checks were now in progress.

The WL-1 project was designed simply to take measurements. It would take them by the hundred thousand during fourteen minutes of flight. It would record data on the missile itself: performance, control, propulsion and guidance systems, trajectory, flight path, velocity, direction change, acceleration, altitude and behavior tendencies in near-vacuum reaches. It would examine conditions and phenomena in the upper atmosphere, and radiation in all layers traversed.

Missile data would be obtained by instrumentation. White Lance was now surrounded by a complex of ballistic, performance, ribbon-frame, and field cameras, by a battery of kinetheodolites and by a network of radar stations slaved to the master Askania that would track White Lance through the first fifty miles of its nine-hundred-mile probe. This data would be of the missile as such. The missile would in turn obtain data of its own workings and of its experience in physical space.

Telemetry, the electronic sounding system within the head component, would record both the data and relay it to ground at every second and every yard of flight. At a peak altitude of nine hundred miles and a peak velocity of eight thousand miles an hour WL-1 would relay signals in the region of one thousand five hundred per second. Just afterward, when the main body and first-stage motor had dropped away, the solid-fuel cuckoo motor would propel the head component vertically downward into the earth's air envelope, and reentry conditions would be examined, relayed, processed, and researched on paper.

Months later, scientific authorities of the Western space organizations would meet at symposia in London, New York, Philadelphia, Rome, Paris, and Frankfurt, to be told in what precise way the hitherto unknown areas of space had now become a little safer for man to explore inside a capsule.

More than usual interest was already being shown in the WL-1 project for two reasons: White Lance had never been flight-tested, and its fuel—HTP/Zenox—had never been used before.

Messages had been coming in to Tokariji for some days now, wishing luck for the trial. Mary White had opened a file for them and it was growing fast. She had shown some of the cables to the P.O. and he had seemed pleased; then with the beginning of Phase 7 there had been no time. She had asked him what kind of reply her staff of three clerks should send. He had said: "Just put 'Thank you. We will do our best.'"

Day 2, Phase 7, was difficult for everyone. The P.O. had arrived late, after his rest. A slight wind had got up and showed no signs of dying yet. And as White Lance was locked into the launcher and the gantry rolled clear, the familiar feeling came again among the personnel: they had passed another stage from which they couldn't go back. They could only go forward; and something, somewhere, might go wrong; one of several thousand tiny transistors might be faulty, a lesion in several miles of hair-fine wire might have gone undetected, an air bubble in the casing of just one of a hundred components might weaken a structure under the stress.

"*We know you'll do it!*" most of the cables had said.

No one could know.

Toward the evening the wind fined down and the sand dust gave less trouble in Area 1. Most of the personnel showed fatigue, nervous rather than physical. They had reached the end of another day but could not rejoice: there was tomorrow.

The ground safety officer came away from the launcher with the last group of technicians and would sign his clearance certificate, he told them, on his way past the P.O.'s office in the Instrumentation Building. As far as could be humanly known, no procedure made during the day had in any way jeopardized safe conditions for tomorrow's schedule. During tonight a guard was being mounted at the launcher, double in strength and supported by the night-shift fire crew for the first time. White Lance was now fully fueled.

Dr. Chapel was in his office preparing the usual conference covering the Day 3, Phase 7, schedule. Irving signed his certificate, without which the conference could not begin. He stayed talking for a few minutes so as to study the P.O. Chapel looked very tired but was obviously well in command of himself. Irving left the building soon after eight o'clock, walking through the twilight to the senior mess.

The Day 3 conference lasted until nearly ten. Phil Whymlett was there the whole time. There was a patch of disagreement on the subject of firing technique with this particular untried missile, but Chapel dealt with it in half an hour and left the atmosphere amicable enough.

At a quarter to midnight Mary was still working in her office, as had been usual for the past week. Three calls had come in for the P.O. and she had successfully located him and made the liaison. The fourth call came in half an hour after the third; it was from Follett, missile officer. He had failed to locate Dr. Chapel. Mary checked her personnel board, tried three numbers and called Follett back.

"Give me another ten minutes, Peter, will you? He's between stations."

During the final phase of a major shoot the P.O. had made a rule that he should be available to any man on any matter at any time, and that his movements should be followed precisely so that he could be located as quickly as possible. But nothing could be done about "between stations," when he was making his way from one building to another and was temporarily out of reach by telephone. The rule therefore prescribed that if he could not be reached within ten minutes at any given time, the P.A. system should be used; there was no part of the establishment where the loudspeakers could not be heard.

Mary put out the first P.A. call at five minutes to midnight, knowing that Follett would also hear it and be reassured that she was tracing Dr. Chapel.

Following the P.A. call several people telephoned Mary on a nonpriority line: Mrs. Chapel, Phil Whymlett, and Dr. Friedmann. They asked her to let them know when the P.O. was located.

At five minutes past midnight she began putting out calls at three-minute intervals. More people began telephoning to say when and where they had last seen Dr. Chapel and she had to ask the switchboard to monitor for her while she kept open the priority line, the one he would use. It did not ring.

Chapter 23

Dr. Chapel's office in the Instrumentation Building was filling up as people came along to wait for the news there. Eve and Phil Whymlett were talking to Mary in her own office while she sat at her desk dealing with the more urgent calls filtering through the monitor screen at the switchboard. The priority line was still silent.

When Mary had a second to spare Whymlett asked: "How long has he been adrift now?"

"Half an hour, Mr. Whymlett."

It gave him a certain sour satisfaction. Ever since Jim had started to bear down heavily on the margins of error in the missile's preparation there had been people who had said, sometimes openly, "If he drives himself into a collapse we'll just have to shoot without him—it might even be an advantage . . ." They had first said it weeks ago, not really meaning it; but later it was felt by some of them that if the principal officer had to be laid off the schedule then a team comprising the missile, area operations, and trials control officers could manage to mount the shoot, with Whymlett— officer in scientific charge—to help them.

Now they knew. The P.O. had been adrift just thirty minutes and a crisis was developing, because not all of the calls piling up at the switchboard were simply enquiries as to the P.O.'s whereabouts; many people—mainly in the scientific groups—didn't care where the hell he was, provided they could talk to him and soon. There were enough technical questions, belatedly arising from the Day 3 conference, to keep Dr. Chapel out of bed for the rest of the night.

At half past twelve the whole island was still wide awake and every light was burning. The security officer was in constant touch with the Instrumentation Building and had organized the police and guard sections into search parties. Tracker dogs were given some of Chapel's belongings to scent and were being taken round the coastline. The main photoflood lamps on the gantry and launcher had been lit and the whole of Area 1 was awash in their glare. Every three minutes the P.A. sounded monotonously:

"Will anyone who knows where Dr. Chapel is please telephone his office immediately, priority line."

It was impossible for a man to get lost on Tokariji, even by night, save in two circumstances: if he were suddenly ill and had fallen somewhere in shadow or if he did not want to be found.

Dr. Friedmann had been twice to Mary's office and had tried to reassure Mrs. Chapel. She was calm, standing at the windows staring out through the pale reflection of her own face; she did not want to talk to anyone. Friedmann quietly asked Phil Whymlett to stay near her, and Whymlett said he would in any case.

It was some ten minutes later when Friedmann saw what should have been obvious to him before and set out from the Instrumentation Building, walking fast, rethinking his impressions of the talks he had had with Chapel last night and this morning. There was only one place where he could have gone. Before Friedmann himself reached there the priority line opened up and Mary answered a call.

Whymlett got out of his chair. Eve turned from the window. People began crowding the door of the P.O.'s office.

Mary had heard this voice before on the telephone but did not recognize it now. It was slow and halting.

"This is Colonel Pyne. Dr. Chapel is with me now. He is perfectly all right. The announcement on your public address system was reported to me, and so I am letting you know."

Mary waited, giving a quick smile and a nod to Mrs. Chapel, but the voice did not go on.

"Thank you, Colonel Pyne, we're most grateful to you."

"He will be leaving here shortly. There is no need for further anxiety."

"I'll pass on the news at once, and—"

Eve had taken the receiver from her. The color had entirely left her face. It seemed difficult for her to speak.

"This is—Mrs. Chapel. My husband is with you?"

"Yes." Carefully he said: "There is absolutely nothing to worry about, Mrs. Chapel. All is in order."

The line went dead.

Pyne had still been in his office when they brought Chapel to him. Unable to sleep and needing urgently to think of what he must do he had told Sergeant Lacey that he would lock up the office himself, and Lacey had turned in. It was just after a quarter past twelve.

The two men were part of the off-duty guard unit. One came in first, leading Chapel; the other followed.

Chapel appeared stunned and glanced about him as if uncertain where he was, or why he was here. His face was bloodless and he seemed to be trembling.

The leading man said: "The prisoner was handed over to me by corporal of the guard, sir, at the blockhouse. Corporal ordered me to escort him to you."

Pyne got up slowly, not able to take his eyes from Chapel. It looked like a case for the M.O.

"The prisoner," he said almost absently, "is Dr. Chapel,

Principal Officer of the civilian establishment, Tokariji. Please refer to him as Dr. Chapel."

"Sir. Corporal says that he was—that Dr. Chapel was trying to—"

The telephone rang and Pyne answered it.

"Guard corporal, sir. Can I make a report?"

"Yes."

"There's Dr. Chapel on his way to you, sir, under escort. I couldn't leave the post so I phoned the guard hut and ordered two men to come here and take him to you, sir. He's on his way now."

Pyne gestured to one of the men to give Chapel a chair, but he wouldn't take it. He was staring now at Pyne, still trembling.

"What happened, Corporal?"

"We was on duty when Dr. Chapel come up and told me he had to inspect the blockhouse, inside. I asked for a signed authority from you, sir, but he just said he was the highest authority in the place and asked me to open the blockhouse for him. He was quite civil, sir, but very determined."

Chapel's eyes suddenly became bright and his voice came sharply—"It *cannot* be allowed to remain there!" He took a pace toward Pyne and one of the men moved quickly, holding his arm.

"Go on, Corporal."

"That's all, sir. I thought it was a matter for you, right away."

"Very good. Dr. Chapel has arrived." He left the telephone and dismissed the guard, locking the door when their footsteps had died away in the passage.

"I wish you'd have a chair. We could both sit down and take it more easily."

Chapel stood stiffly, looking around him again with little jerks of his head. "Why did you lock the door?"

"Because we don't want anyone interrupting us while we talk, do we?"

They stared at each other. Pyne knew that he looked in no better shape than Chapel. Two sleepless nights had followed the day when he had gone to see Hurst, and the decision had still not formed in his mind. It harried him ceaselessly. When Chapel had come in he had been certain that Hurst must have told him, and that this was the inevitable showdown. But Chapel had gone to the blockhouse . . .

"It *must* not be allowed to remain there." It was almost a whisper but with the force of an adamant will behind it. The trembling had stopped and he seemed in full control, even dominating.

Pyne folded his arms and kept his eyes on Chapel. "What made you go there, Dr. Chapel?"

"I don't know." He could remember very little about it. Just as, in the bedroom this morning, he had suddenly found himself standing at the window, he had found himself, tonight, at the blockhouse. All he remembered of his journey there was that a guard had stopped him at the boundary and he had shown him his All Areas pass, which the man had apparently accepted. He could not remember having climbed into the weapon pit. The challenge of the guard had, in a way, awakened him. The darkness—his personal terrifying darkness—had been upon him the whole time, but he was able to suffer it. He was this time *doing* something *in* it— he was not merely lost, engulfed.

But they wouldn't let him see the warhead. He had wanted very urgently to see it, to touch it, and somehow to destroy it, knowing that it was impossible but knowing it must be done. He could not remember all that he had said to the guards; perhaps he was now repeating some of it to Pyne.

"I went there to destroy it. There must be a way. We

ought to exorcise evil. But you won't know what I'm talking about. You are a soldier."

It was very quiet in the little room. Pyne looked at him with his eyes hollowed into his face, his mouth a line of shadow.

Chapel's voice was suddenly pitched sharply—"*You are not concerned.*" He stepped closer to him and Pyne's head lifted an inch, his arms were still folded. Chapel stood stiffly, his hands gripped at his sides with their knuckles pale. His eyes were bright.

"Yes," Pyne told him slowly, "I'm concerned." He turned away, moving behind his desk, because Chapel was ready to hit him and although he could be subdued easily enough it would be undignified and would only make him feel worse. "I've been concerned, Chapel, ever since that hellish thing arrived here." There was no point in telling him everything, how the whole unit had been affected when the rot had set in himself. He'd have to take his word for it. "I am as concerned as you are."

Chapel said nothing. He didn't believe it.

"It could be," said Pyne, "that if things blow up in Malaysia, or Vietnam, or anywhere at all, I would get orders to arm the Triton and fire it. For your information I have already decided that I would disobey such an order." He looked at him again, trying to judge how far he was able to take in what was being said. Chapel looked ill and at the end of his reserves, but perfectly sane. "I'd like you to understand, quite clearly, what I'm saying, Chapel. It's vital. Am I making myself understood?"

"How am I to believe what you say? You are a soldier and committed to war." It was incredible, Pyne thought, how much hate could show itself in a face normally so mild.

"I am also a man, and you should know when a man is speaking the truth." Suddenly he lost patience—"Good God, do I *seem* unconcerned? Are you the only human being sensitive enough to be appalled at the idea of a global nuclear war of attrition with whole continents laid waste and no future afterward for anyone—for *anyone?* Do you think I'm so abysmally unimaginative that I can receive a signal to destroy a city and just say, 'Yes, sir,' and press the button?"

It was he this time who came closer to the other as if to see his face more clearly and read the thoughts in his eyes.

Chapel seemed ready to believe him; the hatred was burning itself out. "You held different views," he said in surprise, "the first time we talked about this."

"That was before I knew. The signal came in later that night. Then I became personally involved."

Someone was in the passage outside, walking quickly. A knock sounded and Pyne called: "Yes?"

"Duty N.C.O., sir!"

"Well?"

"There's a message on the civilian P.A. system, sir. Will anyone seeing Dr. Chapel please telephone his office, priority. Any orders, sir?"

"Thank you. No orders."

The footsteps faded. Pyne said: "They're looking for you." The relief guard had obviously told the duty N.C.O. that Chapel was here. "Do we set their minds at rest?"

Chapel had gone slack and for a moment Pyne thought he was about to fall. Reaction was setting in. He hooked a chair over with his foot and made him sit down; then he went to the desk and dialed the civilian switchboard.

"Dr. Chapel's office please."

They sounded very relieved over there. Then he heard Eve's voice.

"This is—Mrs. Chapel . . ."

She believed as he had believed: that Chapel had been

told. It seemed a small matter now, but she must be reassured.

"All is in order," he told her. She would understand. He rang off before she could say anything more.

Chapel sat untidily in the chair, at a loss. He had been ready to convince Pyne of his error, keep on thrusting until the man saw sense; but Pyne didn't need convincing; there was no need to fight.

"Do you feel up to taking a walk, Chapel?"

His eyes focused with an effort, but he got up. "A walk? Yes."

Pyne found his cap and unlocked the door.

"Then let's go and look at this thing together. The warhead."

Chapter 24

The chief security officer telephoned Colonel Pyne during the morning. The conversation was brief and civil and he made no attempt to nettle Pyne, either because he had no time to spare or because his position was so strong that he need not bother.

"The parade can be arranged for ten o'clock tomorrow morning, if that's convenient for you."

"A full parade?"

"Oh yes. It's only right, you see. They were all there, that time before, and I want them there this time."

"Very well. I have made a note."

"Ten o'clock sharp, then, tomorrow."

Hurst rang off.

Pyne sat thinking. The word he had feared most had not been spoken in the conversation. Apology. He had been frightened of that word for a long time, for nearly all his life, since he was ten or eleven years old and Frisling, the Head, had stood him on the platform in front of the whole school.

"So you are 'sorry,' Pyne? Excellent!"

He and Frisling had simply hated each other from the start, for no reason or for one of those reasons one could never understand; and the Head took pains to humiliate him where a few strokes with a cane would have met the case.

He had even forgotten what precisely he had done to merit the scene on the platform; the scene itself had obliterated all other memories of that time.

"We may therefore put on a cheerful countenance," Frisling had said, "and bask in the righteous glow of your apology."

Laughter came easily to boys in Hall when it was expected of them; it was an age for licking boots.

"And have you nothing else to say, Pyne? Nothing more constructive?"

"I can only say I'm sorry, sir."

"So it appears. One might almost say the record had got stuck."

Much laughter. The herd, following the leader, was rounding on the freak; it was ancient law.

"However." Frisling now addressed the herd itself. "Since Master Pyne says he's *sorry*, we shall have to be content. The rules of Heronfield, sacred though we hold them, can always of course be broken with impunity, providing that one is *sorry*. It's rather convenient."

He had gone on for a longish time, borrowing freely from the Mark Anthony speech and paraphrasing it—Caesar was an *honorable* man.

Pyne had looked down at the sea of faces, listening to the laughter, wanting to run away or shout at the Head, run or fight, one or the other, anything but this withering exposure in public; and the man's voice had tormented him, playing with him, pricking at his susceptibilities as only Frisling knew how, until he couldn't stand it and simply climbed down from the platform to walk up the center aisle of the chairs to the back of the hall, running at last through the big doors as the laughter changed to derisive cheers and someone set them chanting monotonously—*Sorry . . . Sorry . . . Sorry . . .*

Incredible, really, looking back on it; but Frisling must have been a past master at rousing the mob, the type who would have done well in Nazi Germany. Of course it had all been a great joke and one had to take it like a man and all that. In a few days everyone else had forgotten the whole thing and his own few friends appeared to be his friends again, as if nothing had happened.

But something had happened.

There were many ways of evading the obligation to apologize and he became adept very fast. It was easier still in the army, especially as an officer. One was not entitled to make formal apology to a superior, since it implied a personal relationship that was not officially permissible; nor did one apologize to a subordinate. His brother officers got used to him and put it down to lack of moral fiber in one small respect.

It had never bothered him, until now; and even now it was going to make precious little difference.

An hour after the telephone call from Hurst he sent for Nash. The heat was intense today; the small wind had died in the night and the sun struck the rock of Tokariji like a brass fist.

Nash found him sitting behind his desk, looking very businesslike despite the hollowness of his eyes and the lines that had tightened during the last few days around his mouth. The desk was filled with paperwork, most of it spilling from the "Out" tray.

"Robert." He signed a report and put it with the rest. "I am mounting a special night exercise at 21.00 hours and I want the following men mustered in readiness half an hour beforehand." He was already making a list from memory. "Knapper . . . Blythe . . . Scott—is Scott back on duty now?"

"Yes, sir."

"Right. Malinson . . . Jones . . . Brockway . . ."

He wrote fast but legibly.

Nash wanted to ask if there had been a signal in, but Ken didn't look too ready for questions. Something had happened; he didn't know what. They said Dr. Chapel had been missing last night and had shown up here; it must be to do with that. He wished Ken would knock off a whole complete bloody bottle and hit the bed. He couldn't go on like this.

"West . . . Driburg . . . And Company Sergeant-major Rice in charge of party." He reached and pulled open a drawer and slapped an envelope on the desk. "Special orders for you, to be opened at 24.00 hours tonight."

Nash put the envelope into his wallet. It bore the regimental seal in fresh wax.

"This is a secret-mission exercise, Robert." He did not look up from the desk. "It has to go like clockwork. Please send the C.S.M. here right away, then go and brief these men."

"Right, sir. Am I in on this one?"

"Not in the first stage of the operation. You'll be commanding the second stage according to your sealed orders."

The missile-recovery launch had left Tokariji at 21.30 hours and was still on course at cruising speed an hour later, her position some twenty-three sea miles due south of the island. The ocean was calm. The aging moon had risen not many minutes ago, yellowing the water eastward.

Pyne was standing aft of the helmsman, watching the saffron wake and the black object humped in the stern. It was in two sections. Dr. Chapel had given precise instructions on the use of the spoiling mechanism, and the thing was already harmless: even if it were now armed with the catalystic detonator it would remain inactive. Immersion in salt water would render it no more dangerous than a lump of rock, even if the ocean-bed currents brought the two sections together. According to the charts, the ocean bed in this area was seventy fathoms below, part of the underwater mountainside the peak of which was Tokariji, and the two sections would be unsalvageable.

"Heave to, bo'sun!"

The throb of the engines died. Sergeant-major Rice came aft from the bow to await orders; he had been briefed simply to have the solid-fuel motor taken from the blockhouse and put on board the launch; there had been no explanation nor any mission objective for the exercise.

Colonel Pyne was for the moment silent. The launch floated with the engines shut off. There was no sea running, and no question of anchoring.

Pyne was gazing at the two black sections with their bright orange bands. Chapel had not understood all the implications last night when they had gone to the blockhouse together but had been moved to a vague surprise. The door had been shut and they had stood together looking at the warhead. Pyne had told him briefly:

"I need your help technically. Is it possible to make this thing permanently harmless and sink it off the coast?"

Chapel had been slow to understand but he was on to the technicalities at once, describing what would need to be done. It seemed very simple to Pyne. "In any case the half-life is less than two years, in the primary component."

"What about radioactivity spreading on the sea bed?"

"There would be a minimal discharge, and decomposition would be accelerated by the submarine mineral constituents. Was it an academic question, Pyne?"

"No. I am going to dump it."

"I don't understand you."

"You don't have to. The idea's been on my mind for some days now, and it links up with other things." He turned to the door but Chapel stopped him.

"This is on your own initiative?"

"Yes."

"Won't it mean trouble for you? A prison term?"

"Probably." He looked into Chapel's eyes and saw that they were perfectly rational. "When I have dumped it, I shall telephone you. I shall merely say that action has been taken. You will know what I mean."

"I wish I could understand you, Pyne."

"All you have to understand is that by midnight tomorrow there will no longer be a nuclear warhead on this island. Meanwhile I would ask you to treat this as highly confidential."

He had walked with Chapel as far as the living quarters where a small crowd of people had gathered to wait for him.

He had seen to the mechanism himself early this morning. It was a matter of removing the blanking plugs from the inner main cell and inhibiting the ducts with mineral oil. The catalyst detonator was stored apart, and he had taken it to the shore in the afternoon, breaking the sensitized diaphragm and throwing it into the sea.

The warhead had been split by the technical section of the party he had chosen, and the two components were still in the slings that had lifted them onto the launch.

"Sar' major."

"Sir?"

"Jettison the motor, both sections."

Rice looked at the humped shapes and back at Colonel Pyne. "Jettison, sir? Overboard?"

"Overboard." The C.S.M. was taking too long about it. "Smartly!"

"Sir! *Forward party!*"

The winches were designed to recover Javelin 33s with fuel discharged, and a body of men was needed to handle these heavier components as the slings rose clear of the deck. There was no hitch. Within ten minutes the launch was riding higher on the water and the slings dangled empty.

The launch made harbor a little before 23.45 hours. Most of the civilian establishment was still awake and lights burned throughout the Instrumentation Building. Pyne gave a last order to the C.S.M.

"Take what men you need and lower the Triton to prone position and spread the pit camouflage. Dismiss the block-house guard."

"Yes, sir."

Pyne looked around at the party of men. Their faces were indistinct in the moonlight but he knew them, every one.

As Sergeant-major Rice got them to attention and turned them for marching he heard the C.O. say quietly:

"The operation was most efficiently carried out, and I thank you."

Captain Stoner had been playing snooker with Wilson most of the evening, surrendering the table only three times and going across to the senior mess for more beer in the intervals, then coming back to continue what had turned out to be a marathon challenge tournament.

Wilson saw Nash twice on his way about the camp and asked him what was on, because there was some talk of a special exercise Ken had mounted with the C.S.M. Nash wasn't communicative. "It's a special exercise, is all I know."

Soon after eleven o'clock Wilson turned in, having had more beer than he'd meant, and Stoner wrote some letters until midnight. He was putting on his pajamas when Nash gave an odd kind of knock at the door of his room and came in.

Stoner looked at him and said: "Christ. What's happened?"

Nash had a completely blank face and looked ill as hell. He was holding the doorway for support and it was a minute before he could speak.

"Ken's shot himself."

Chapter 25

He telephoned Dr. Chapel as arranged. There was nothing left to be done. His desk was cleared and the two messages written.

The shape of the Triton had gone from the skyline when he got into the Land-Rover and drove along the east road; the men's voices called; they were spreading the camouflage. It was a gesture to Chapel: he must have hated seeing the Triton standing there.

He drove beyond the first outcrop of rock so that the sound of the shot would not alarm the camp and stopped the car, sitting for a few minutes to watch the moon's path across the ocean.

The whisky burned in his stomach; he had drunk the whole flaskful in his room after telephoning. For courage? No one would know.

It might have been all right if no one had known; but Hurst knew. You couldn't make a gentleman's agreement with a man like that; even if the company were paraded and the apology gone through with, it wouldn't end. Hurst had power over him and could reach out for him wherever he was. Why wait for that? *I can finish you off. Career, reputation, all chance of a decent future. Wipe you up. Okay?*

The breeze made patches of dark across the moon's path. *We are an operational unit away from home and we are of-*

fered a hospitality that it would be easy to abuse. Any member of this unit, of whatever rank, found in the vicinity of the civilian women's quarters will become subject to the most severe disciplinary action.

The whisky burned; a good friend, loyal to the last.

We have been accepted here for what we are—a company of gentlemen, and as such we shall one day leave here, with our good name intact.

He unclipped the holster. It was time to stop thinking.

Was it worth it, for you?

I don't know, Eve. I don't mind this. It wasn't only you.

You mean you refuse to make a simple apology?

I do.

Frisling, whatever made them put you in charge of the tender young?

Your orders will be to destroy the city of Peking.

No, damn you. Just Kenneth Pyne.

The wind shifted across the water and the bright path began slowly breaking up.

Nash had opened his sealed orders at 24.00 hours.

My dear Robert: the second stage of tonight's operation will be tiresome for you. I regret to say that the pressure of many circumstances has obliged me to end my life. Please take a stretcher party and transport along the perimeter track eastward, where you will find me in the car. I understand that the civilian establishment is to conduct the White Lance trial the day after tomorrow, and in case the event of my death should disturb anyone I require it to be treated as secret information until the trial is over. For safety's sake I should confine all ranks to camp for this period. Enclosed are two messages, the first to be dispatched to the War Office; it gives my reasons for this act, which were the mounting agonies of mind on the subject of my responsibilities as commander of

*this unit, the details of which I confided in you against or-
ders. Please see that the second message is given directly into
the hand of Chief Security Officer, Tokariji, by name Hurst.
For your information, the device stored in the weapon-pit
blockhouse was tonight submerged in deep ocean on my orders, the natural consequences of which I am not prepared to
suffer. There is of course no responsibility applicable to anyone else in the unit. I would count it a personal favor if you
would let it be known I cherished at all times the privilege
of commanding such men as you now have with you. Your
own loyalty and understanding, Robert, was a source of
strength to me, but even you could not prevent the inevitable.
I wish you well. Ken.*

Company Sergeant-major Rice was bringing his party up
from the weapon pit when he saw Major Nash run out of
the office section and start up the nearest transport, swinging
it onto the perimeter road eastward.

Nash drove fast on a cold engine, not thinking any particular thoughts, just seeing Ken's face. Words came into his
mind monotonously—*Not true . . . Not true . . .* The head-
lights played among the rocks and drew shadows from
them that danced blackly as the car bounced across the dips.
He had to drive this fast in order to get to the other side
of something beyond which Ken would be dead. If he could
get there soon, Ken would be alive. He understood this
clearly but not in so many words; it was a state of awareness
that had the shape of dread.

He found the C.O.'s personal transport parked with the
side-lights on, coming upon it suddenly where the track
turned sharply past an outcrop. He stayed only long enough
to make sure and then drove slowly back through the dust
haze that had still not settled from the journey out. After
what seemed a very long time he was knocking on Stoner's
door.

Chapter 26

By six o'clock Mary was in her office and closing the blinds as the sun came out of the ocean and the wall glowed red. She changed the schedule panel to read Day 6 Phase 7 but nobody would look at it because everyone knew what day it was. The White Lance shoot was ordered for 21.00 hours, one hour later than last night and four hours before the moon rose.

By eight o'clock two of Mary's relief clerks came in and took over the monitoring desk; the messages already beginning to reach the Instrumentation Building were to be monitored, edited, and collated with the help of the master tape recorder linked with the three telephones so that whenever Dr. Chapel passed through his office he could check at a glance the minute-by-minute situation as the day progressed.

A third clerk stood by the personnel-location board with an extension telephone; as each key technician and scientist left one place and made for another someone would call Extension 9 and the board would be changed. Mary was too busy now to do it the normal way.

The priority line was open only for calls establishing actual targets reached in the schedule and for urgent information of whatever kind. The other two lines were handling location queries and transmission of technical reports. Mary and the

Extension 9 clerk wore switchboard-type headsets to save time.

"Kine 3—having difficulty setting up cross-references till the slaving's effected—how long now, please?"

"Radar Control: when can we start slaving?"

"Twelve noon with luck but I'll let you know when we're set."

"Kine 3: by twelve noon, maybe earlier, let you know."

"Mary, where's Len Johns got to for God's sake—the board hasn't pegged him!"

"Try Area 1, launcher or gantry."

"Priority? Doppler network rigged and final checks tick-Toka. Standing by."

"P.O. wanted in Area 2 for approval prelim. slaving—when can be done?"

"He's Area 1. Call him direct please."

"Met. conditions unchanged for 21.00."

"Priority: Emergency power system final-checked and ready for switching."

"Mary, tell Jock at Kine 5 we're fixing the beam at 190 and 13 degrees, repeat please—"

"One hundred ninety and 13 degrees, thank you, Steve."

"The P.O. has just left Area 1 on his way to Area 2 for prelim. slaving check."

The clerk changed the board. Chapel to Area 2. Follett to gantry. Brayworth to main Doppler post. Whymlett to Instrumentation. MacClure to launcher.

Outside the building the sun beat down through the windless air, its light flashing on the movement of antennae and the traffic plying among the network of installations. White Lance towered, shining, beside the thin mast of the launcher. A Met. balloon was rising against the blank blue sky.

Dr. Chapel came back to Area 1 just before noon to supervise the final checks to the release jacks and umbilical mast gear. For the first time today the ground safety officer gave him no more than a glance. It was a miracle, and Irving had been observing it for thirty-six hours now, and all he had said to Dr. Friedmann was: "It's a miracle."

"And is it a safe miracle?"

"I've checked it. It's safe. I certify. What did you do?"

"Nothing. It happened."

Chapel looked fatigued. It showed in his face but not in his movements. It was the fatigue of a long-distance runner whose powers are being strained to the limit but who will last the race because he still has untapped reserves.

No one knew what had happened to him but those who had time to think about it at all believed it was simply that on the night when he was missing he had had some kind of nervous breakdown that had purged him and set him up again. It was all they needed to believe. No one connected the change in him with the fact that if one looked eastward across the ridge of excavated earth one could no longer see the shape of the army Triton that had been part of the landscape for two months.

There was only, now, the question of what White Lance would do and that was the question they had worked with and slept with for weeks. WL-1 was unpredictable and carried an untried fuel of unmeasured potency. It was a question that had become almost dear to them and they would be lost without it. Tonight they would find the answer and right or wrong they would find it for themselves.

Many people had nothing to do today. Their work was finished and they would not be called on again until zero. One by one, scores of installations and systems had been coming into final phase during the past few days and now stood idle and waiting. Their crews and operators chain-smoked in safe areas or chewed gum at the fringe of the launcher section, trying to find something to say and someone to listen. Nobody said much and nobody listened.

The chief security officer stood watching the frenzy of

work in Area 1, and sometimes saw Mrs. Chapel at the edge of the group where the P.O. was moving from place to place. Once he saw her, neat in her overalls, with a tray of tea, and the group stopped milling for a ten-minute break to drink a cup, and Hurst was pleased with the scene, knowing the power he had and would not use.

He did not understand what had got into the mind of Colonel Pyne; it was his regret; he'd like to know what went on in everyone's mind; it was his job.

Pyne had said in his brief note: *I have given orders that the incident of my death shall remain a matter of secrecy until after White Lance has undergone its trials, so that concentration among the civilian personnel shall not be affected, however slightly, at so critical a time. As this incident in no way involves security you will perhaps keep the knowledge of it to yourself for this short period. I shall also hope that you may find it in you to respect the wishes of the dead, in these most relevant circumstances, and allow that no harm shall befall those persons whom I have wronged. I have no claim on you in this but surely you could not do otherwise than profit spiritually in granting this last wish. K. M. Pyne.*

But it didn't make sense; there had never been any question. He had told the man himself: if he'd wanted to break people he wouldn't know where to start . . . In his job he got hold of a lot of information, especially in a small place like Tokariji! Besides, he had respect for Dr. Chapel. Pyne couldn't see things like that, and he'd obviously been going troppo anyway. All he'd been asked to do was apologize . . .

He watched the scene as Mrs. Chapel took the tray of tea round, smiling to her husband. None of them knew. Only he knew, and it was a feeling of power that he had over them. When you've got power, you don't want to use it. You keep it, and add to it, pile it up. Oh, there were a lot of things a fellow like Pyne would never see.

He moved away to watch them bringing up the big launcher screen to Area 2.

If a man couldn't say he was sorry, if he'd rather die than say he was sorry, what sort of a man could he be? He'd never understand, and that was his only regret.

The sky screen blocked half the nearest building, and a bunch of technicians began signaling Instrumentation for naked-eye bearings. Another hydrogen balloon was lifting from the Met. area, bright silver in the sun.

The P.A. sounded. After this time, 13.00 hours, no traffic will be allowed on the slip road between Areas 1 and 2. Transport of crews and gear must be made by Diesel loaders only. Repeating . . .

By midafternoon the final-check reports were coming into the Instrumentation Building without a pause, and Dr. Chapel went to his own telephone to deal with them.

Toward evening the emergency fire and ambulance crews brought up their vehicles and equipment into the launch area and the ground safety officer conferred with their leaders. Soon afterward a kennelman began taking the guard dogs away into the safety areas and leashing them behind cover. The P.A. was broadcasting the final-phase series of instructions to all personnel as the sun lowered to one diameter across the sea.

At nightfall a helicopter took off for 'Covery Island with a briefing team on board. On Tokariji the lights came on and the launch area froze white under the photofloods.

At 20.00 hours conditions of emergency standby were announced over the P.A. and a few minutes afterward the personnel began leaving the launch area. With one hour to go, Dr. Chapel took his trials team into the Control Center.

At 20.30 hours—zero minus 30—White Lance stood alone, supported by the thin stem of the launcher mast. It would not be touched again by a human hand. Shimmering in the glare of a million watts it stood tall in the night, slim, beautiful, and immeasurably dangerous. The doors and escape hatches in the Control Center blockhouse were sealed and braced from the inside against high-pressure blast at zero minus 15. The G.S.O. had come in and was standing alone with nothing more to do. He looked very tired. The flight safety officer took over from him automatically; they had not even glanced at each other.

At zero minus 9 Dr. Chapel turned his head and saw the *Missile Active* sign light up on the master console panel. It was followed over the minutes by the prelim. sequence lights, blue, yellow, and green. If a red light came on the sequence would automatically stop. Everyone began watching for a red light among the hundred indicators.

The P.A. warning of zero minus 7 brought the instrumentation system into slaved focus on the missile: bore-sight, spectral cines, Minitrack, photometers, Baker-Nunn and Contrave kines, ballistic, performance, and calibration cameras.

Minus 6. All screens functioning. Radar remote and tracking displays set for zero. Impact predictors lining up with automatic beaming to 'Covery.

Minus 4. Command links established. Telemetry standing by. Acoustic recording network showing green.

Minus 1. The sequence officer looked at the T.C.O. The missile systems showed green. The flight safety officer checked all panels for red. There was no red light showing anywhere.

Dr. Chapel listened to the central timing unit for ten more seconds and then nodded to the sequence officer.

They began the countdown. It was heard, muted, in the Control Center. It was heard in every building in Tokariji. It sounded across the silent launch area where the missile stood, where there was no one to hear.

The sequence officer looked once more at Chapel, who gave a final nod. The switch was thrown.

The automatic firing circuit was activated. Only the indicators showed that the missile was in live sequence. Pressure was building up in the ground start and flight tanks. There was no sound in the launch area until the cooling water burst from the jets in the duct below the missile. Movement came suddenly in the vision prisms as the umbilical conduit was severed and snaked down across the trampoline grid.

Men began speaking.

"Program motors running."

"Cameras on."

"Acoustics on."

"Pre-heat starting."

"Gyros uncaged."

"Fifty per cent specified minimum thrust."

Then the ground-start circuit closed down and the gush of steam below the missile clouded into the duct where the cooling water foamed white in the glare of the photofloods. Two small explosions threw off the cooling tubes from the missile.

At automatic zero the HTP/Zenox motor came in and the gush of steam became tinged with crimson as the thrust increased to full specified minimum and the sound began rolling across the island.

White Lance moved.

"Missile away."

The movement was slow. An exhaust cloud gathered to a freak wind and passed across the vision panels and when it had cleared there was a gap between the tail fins and the launcher base, and fire burned there. The shadow of the missile drew across the area, gathering speed. The sound of a tempest surged across the land and across the ocean and White Lance moved less slowly as the bright flame lengthened beneath and colored the night and the island red.

Into some of the men who watched, terror came, and they accommodated it, knowing they must. Those at the control consoles were not affected; they could not watch the missile; they must watch the indicators and cathode screens, examining the body, systems, and nerves of the missile as it broke free of the earth; but into those who watched White Lance itself the terror came, because they witnessed a thing that the vestigial animal brain in man had not yet learned to look upon unmoved.

Thrusting in tumult from the heart of its own storm, its great length shot with the colors of inferno against the black of night, it stood for this little time in dominance over the island in the sea, shrinking all else to insignificance—man, building, and the rock itself—as it lorded the elements, a god from a volcano loosed against the stars. Its voice alone was terror-bringing; it was the cry of the hurricane.

Already its identity was changing as it gathered strength, lifting faster with each second, its shape losing the colors of its own fire and merging with the dark until the quadruple streams of exhaust flame and the tail-fin beacons alone were visible. The sound remained, bellowing horizonward and drumming in the earth beneath men's feet, but the missile was now a glow of light, a new star in the firmament.

In the Control Center blockhouse the console panels had become alive and speech was no longer possible; the floor shook and the air itself felt solid against the ears. Whymlett, standing near the master cathode where the track of the missile crept, felt his skull vibrating to the shock of the sound that beat against the walls.

He watched Jim Chapel, who was motionless, his head held still and slightly tilted, his eyes alone flicking along the indicator panels and flicking back, reading off the flight conditions as the missile drove through the five thousand feet altitude sector and settled into predicted trajectory.

Nowhere did a red light come on. The *Destroy* panels remained dark. The flight safety officer scanned the consoles with his eyes calm, the destruction switch within inches of his right hand, as yet untouched.

Voices began coming in against the diminishing roar.

"Plus 50. Nine thousand feet. Stable."

Radar had locked on. Sky screens were shutting down.

"Plus 100. Eighty thousand feet. Velocity five thousand m.p.h. Stable."

Quietness came gradually. The image was small now on the cathode screens.

"Plus 150. Altitude seven hundred miles. Velocity six thousand. Approaching apogee. Stable."

Whymlett turned away suddenly, his body aching from enforced stillness. It was going to be all right. He looked at Jim. Jim had not moved. His hands were held in the pockets of his jacket, at rest.

"Flame-out—flame-out, sir."

"Yes," Chapel said.

Eight hundred miles above Tokariji the new star had vanished. White Lance was riding on empty tanks, still thrusting at near-vertical trajectory on momentum alone. For minutes the missile would proceed on course toward its nine-hundred-mile apogee, a dark alien object adrift in the magnetosphere, until ground command turned it through a hundred and seventy degrees and the solid-fuel motor was ignited.

For the first time Chapel moved, wandering from one console to the next, checking the figures, comparing the flight data that was streaming in from the computer net as the instrumentation kept track of the missile.

A man stood back from his console, took a handkerchief and wiped his neck. The F.S.O. turned away from the destruction switch and folded his arms.

Outside the blockhouse the all-clear sirens were sounding across the island.

On 'Covery the men waited, standing in groups, facing the east.

The sky was starry and the ocean black. In every direction

lay black water, glassy and soundless; the island seemed afloat in it.

"*Stage two firing. Stand by reentry optics.*"

The men looked into the sky and saw nothing. From the signals on the P.A. they knew that the first stage had separated and that the second stage was still up there close on a thousand miles high and was now tilted through 170 degrees and pointed earthward. They knew that the stage two solid-fuel motor had just fired and was at this instant thrusting the head component downward at four thousand m.p.h., so that it could experience velocity conditions as it plunged into the atmospheric envelope and recorded its findings.

"*Prediction Zone Four. Will impact Zone Four.*"

They knew that they would see the brightness of White Lance as it burned into the atmosphere, transmitting its signals through the incandescent casing in the last few minutes of its life. They knew that they would hear the impact on the rocks of the fourth zone here on 'Covery.

But there was nothing to be seen in the sky.

"*Impact imminent. Zone Four.*"

The instruments were set in motion automatically; camera shutters opened to record the flare of the missile; acoustic systems were set to record the sound of the impact and the wave of smaller explosions that would follow as the rain of fragments hit ground.

"*Final warning: impact imminent. Zone Four.*"

The men moved to the blast-proof shelters. They did not talk; they felt that a wrong word might break the great fortune that was theirs, so fragile was it.

White Lance was to die, to burn its way down from the stars and smash upon rock most terribly; but its multiple thousand signals would have been received and the data recorded for analysis. Men would have no more use for the messenger.

233

They stood outside the shelters and stared upward. White Lance was coming to 'Covery.

"*Zone Four. Zone Four. Zone Four.*"

Dead overhead the light began flaring among the stars. It grew very bright, flowing across the sea and touching the rocks alive with an unearthly brilliance. The men, their eyes more used to darkness, could no longer look at it. The whole sky burned.

They went into the shelters and stood with clenched hands, afraid and unashamed of their fear.

The terrain outside was ablaze with acid light.

"*Impacting Zone Four. Impacting. Impacting.*"

White Lance fell from the night and the peak of the ocean mountain shook to its dying.